DOG-EARED DANGER

ST. MARIN'S COZY MYSTERY SERIES - BOOK 11

ACF BOOKENS

1

For long periods of my life, I had imagined I'd always be on my own until I died, surrounded by good friends, but lacking that partner to talk through the challenges of the daily with. Now, though, here I was, mulching around the hundreds of crocus leaves that were just beginning to appear in what would be my yard in just a few short days, a yard I was tending with my fiancé Jared.

My fiance. Just the thought of that made me smile as I carefully bounced the pitchfork and let the brown pine bark mulch bounce down around the emerging bulbs. Jared and I had planted almost one thousand bulbs in the fall with the idea that we'd have a blooming show in the yard for the wedding, which was just ten days away. The ceremony was going to be there, in the backyard, and if the weather stayed warm and sunny, the purple, yellow, and white flowers would do most of the decorating for us.

That is if the two of us didn't collapse from exhaustion before the wedding. Jared had been promoted to sargeant at the police force, and my bookstore, All Booked Up, was getting busier by the way. Both things were amazing, especially since they meant that our wedding expenses were covered and we were able to do what we had decided, as a couple, was most important to us – give generously when our funds would really help.

Often, this meant they simply gave cash to people suffering from homelessness or providing money for a hotel when a family was forced out by fire. We added another micro-loan through Kiva each month, and that was rewarding. But our dream was to help even more people, particularly when housing was a need, and we had visions of buying the land behind our house and putting up tiny houses that could be temporary homes for people who needed a place to land while they got back on their feet.

Well, that and to fund the local animal shelter as much as possible, seeing as we were both big animal lovers and had two dogs and a rather grumpy cat named Aslan. We had even talked of getting a puppy for a bit, but that idea had been short-lived when we remembered just how busy our lives already were and just how often a puppy needed to piddle.

I filled my last wheelbarrow load full of mulch and dumped it around the live oak out front before spreading it and then parking the wheelbarrow against the side of the house. I was too tired to even think about putting it away properly. That would have to wait until my day off. Now, though, I needed to get to work. After a shower, a long, hot shower.

MAYHEM, my hound dog, and Taco, my basset hound, had already tuckered themselves out playing in the backyard, and when I called them to make the walk of a few blocks to work, they heaved themselves to standing as if they were elephants just waking from a 12-hour nap. Soon, though, they were toddling along and sniffing every single thing on the way to the store as if they hadn't sniffed exactly the same things twice a day, almost every day, for a month now. I guess dog noses didn't get bored.

These two were the best of friends to each other and to me, and today, I was going to give them a surprise. But first, we had to open the bookstore, and at this rate, we were going to arrive at closing. I gently tugged on their leads and picked up my pace. Fortunately, Taco must have been tired enough to comply but not too tired to walk. Otherwise, he'd simply lay down and stay there, his center of gravity so low that no amount of coercing could move him against his will. It wasn't an uncommon thing for Jared – and sometimes me – to carry the lazy dog home after a long walk.

We reached the front door of the store with not a minute to spare before opening. Typically, I got in early and spent some time putting the store in order, caffeinating, and setting things up, but lately, I'd just been too busy to get her that early. I flung open the door, flipped on the neon sign, and released the dogs to their usual lap around the shop.

I could smell coffee brewing from Rocky's café and didn't even stop to put down my bag or leashes before heading her way. I knew it wasn't good for me to drink as much caffeine as I had been, but I wasn't going to make it without some help.

Rocky saw me coming, pulled a triple shot into the very large travel mug I kept under her counter and then added plenty of vanilla before steaming the rest up with milk. I only had to stand at the counter for a few seconds before she handed me my drink and said, "Good morning. How are things?" She was studying my face, and I wasn't sure why.

"Good morning. Things are good, busy, but really good." I looked at her, and she was sort of squinting at me now. "Why?" I asked, trying to keep the edge out of my voice and barely succeeding. I was so tired.

"You're too tired, Harvey. You need to rest more. Can you do that?" My friend was leaning far over the counter, her eyes holding mine.

I sighed and slumped beside her on the counter. "I don't think so," I said. "There's just so much to do."

Rocky put her hand on Harvey's arm. "Let us help," she said. "You and Jared are going to make yourselves sick doing all this, and then you won't even enjoy your hard work."

"You guys have already helped enough." I was so bad at accepting help, mostly because I'd grown up thinking that I was only a burden to most people.

"Nope, no we have not." She pushed off the counter. "I'm sending out the book signal."

I smiled and sighed. "Okay," I said as I picked up my latte and headed back to the bookstore.

The "book signal" was the term that my friends had made up for the group texts I sent when I wanted to communicate with all of them at one time. We made potluck dinner plans and sent SOS's for each other. Now, Rocky was going to mobilize everyone to help with the wedding. I was almost teary with gratitude.

While I tidied the store and restocked our bags, I could see Rocky tapping away on her phone between customers. She was talking a lot, and I couldn't imagine what they were saying. This time, though, my friends had kept me off the group text, so I had no idea what was going on. I decided that was probably a good thing and headed over to the fantasy section to straighten things up. We'd just started a YA fantasy book group, and those kids (and adults, too) were pouring through our collection. I'd already had to reorder *The Fragile Threads Of Power*, V.E. Schwab's latest, twice, and it was looking like we'd need to fill that order again. The book was so good, so I couldn't blame them.

For the next couple hours, I straightened shelves and pulled returns, placed an order for more books, and even had time to dust a little bit. It was quiet. But about 11am, I heard the murmur of voices outside, and soon, almost all of my friends were in the middle of the bookstore, huddled around my mom.

I smiled and then walked over. "What's happening here?"

"Nothing you need to worry about," Mom said. "We've got this."

"Got what?" I said, playing dumb.

"Got you," my friend Stephen said as he stepped forward and hugged me. "Rocky, Mart, and your mom have pulled together a list of tasks that need to be completed before your wedding, and we are your street team."

I glanced around, but I didn't see any sign of Mart. "Is Mart coming?"

"Oh no," my friend Cate said as she sidled up to me and bumped my hip. "She's engineering all of this from the winery." Cate smiled. "But she'll be here later."

"Your mom is right, though," our friend Elle said. "We've got this."

"I'm in charge of decorations," Pickle, one of the actual good 'good ole boys' said and then winked at me.

Mom smacked his arm. "Stop that. Do not stress the bride." She turned to me. "Now, don't the pups have an appointment today?"

I looked at my watch. "Oh right. Their spa day. I'd better get them over there."

Dad strolled over and grabbed the dogs leashes from the hook behind the counter. "I'll go with you then take you to lunch."

"Great plan," my assistant manager Marcus said. "I've got the store."

I wanted to protest, to assert that I didn't need all this attention and pampering because that was what Southern women did – refuse help - but honestly, I was too tired to even mount a small grumble. So I took Mayhem's leash from my dad, attached it to the tail-wagging creatures now at my feet, and followed Taco and Dad out the door.

This spa day had been Jared's idea originally. He was worried that the dogs were feeling our stress and thought they might need a bit of pampering to help keep them calm until the wedding. I had loved the idea but for different reasons: our dogs stank, and I wanted them smelling like spring flowers for the event. I had to admit, now though, that Jared was on to something. . . I just wished I had time to get a spa day in for myself.

The new doggy spa and daycare in town was called Doggy Dos, and while I felt like maybe the words *doggy* and *do* conjured up a different images than fur styling, I did want to support new businesses in town. Besides, their front entrance was so cute with the cartoonishly large animated fire hydrant and the manicured "facilities" that they had installed in the alley next to the shop. I hadn't seen grass that green except at a putt-putt course.

A mechanical woofing sound went off as we walked in, and within a moment, a young woman with a gorgeous tattoo of a butterfly on her sternum said, "How can I help?"

I walked toward her as I took Taco's leash from Dad. "I booked these two in for a full spa day. Mayhem and Taco," I said as she began to tap on the screen.

"Oh yes," she said with a smile. "They're here for the Scrub and Fluff, the Puppycure, and the Canine Cuddle." She looked at the dogs. "You two are also in luck. Our new Reiki practitioner is here for her first day. If you don't mind," the woman said looking at me, "we'll get them with her, too."

I could feel Dad bristle just a bit beside me. Reiki and acupuncture, anything not pretty typically Western in its health approach, was suspect to my dad. But I was learning to keep an open mind. "Sure," I said. "As long as the person is qualified."

My dad looked at me and raised his eyebrows as he mouthed *qualified?*

"Oh yes," the woman said. "She's been working in veterinary offices around Virginia for years. She knows what she's doing."

The young woman pulled a red book out from below the counter and said, "Can I just get your contact info and payment information? We'll get that all squared and have a receipt for you when you pick the pups up."

"Of course," I said as I pulled my wallet out and handed her my credit card before sharing my address and phone number.

"Perfect," she said as she closed the book and came around the counter to kneel down and greet her guests. "It's nice to meet you Taco and Mayhem." She looked up to me to be sure she had applied the right name to the right pooch.

I smiled and nodded before giving the pups a scratch myself. "When should I come back for them?"

"5pm is great. But you might want to bring the car. Bassetts, as I'm sure you know, are ruthless when they're determined not to move. And these two are going to be puppy puddles when you come back." She smiled at me as I handed her the leashes.

"Great tip," I said. "Thanks."

Dad and I walked back out onto the street as my dogs followed their new friend without a moment's hesitation. I figured there must use treat-scented air freshener to lure them back, either that or the dogs knew they were about to be spoiled.

"Please do not tell me that you asked that woman if their dog Reiki specialist was qualified. How could you possibly be qualified to wave her arms over people, I mean dogs and do anything?"

I sighed. "Dad, I don't know how all this works, but I do know that when I've had Reiki done, I feel better. But also, people who know the practice say you need to be careful who works on you. If I need to be careful, I need to be careful with my dogs, too." I added this last bit because I knew it would push Dad's button a little. He had gotten better about seeing dogs as more than dirty creatures who should live outside all the time. When it came to his own dog Sidecar, he was practically treating that pooch like a human child. But he still couldn't quite break through the belief that you didn't pamper an animal.

To his credit and probably because Mom had put the fear of God into him about stressing me out, he let the subject drop, and we headed over to Chez Cuisine, our favorite place for lunch because I could get the owner Max's famous risotto, which I LOVED, and Dad could get escargot, which I couldn't even watch him eat. Still, it was our tradition – he called me boring, and I called him gross... and we caught up a bit.

We'd just placed our order with our waitress when a group of three women, including the young woman from the dog spa, came in and got a table next to us. I smiled at the woman who had taken Mayhem and Taco.

"They're doing great," she said with a big smile. "Taco has quite a snore."

I laughed. "That he does," I said. "Thanks for taking such good care of them."

The young woman started to reply to me, but the woman to her right with a severe streak of white running through her carefully-styled hair said, "Caro, we are in a meeting" and pulled Caro by the arm until she sat down.

"You're staring, Harvey," Dad said as he took a sip of his water.

"That woman just kind of assaulted her employee," I said as I turned my eyes to him.

"What?" he said as he started to push back his seat.

"No, it's okay. She just pulled on her arm. They seem alright now ." I didn't want to make a scene over something that Caro herself might have not been bothered by, and besides, I could still see their table if something else happened.

Dad and I chatted about the wedding, about his consulting business, and Mom's many, many charity events while we enjoyed our lunch and decided to split a crème brulee. We were just about to tap the sugar on the top when the voices from the table next to us got very loud.

I looked up to see the older woman leaning forward so far that she was spitting into Caro's face as she shouted and pumped one fist in the air. "Hurt your feelings. If this is how you are going to act, then I don't think this position is going to work out for you. I can't believe you're being so overly-sensitive." Her voice was getting louder, and her fist beat the air more vehemently with each word.

Dad was just about to stand up when I heard Max, someone who had surprisingly become a very dear friend, say, "Madame, we do not tolerate abusive behavior of any sort in this establishment." His voice was even but firm.

"Abusive?" The woman rolled her eyes. "You need to stay out of what you don't understand." She had lowered her voice a little but not much.

"Ma'am, I'm afraid I have to ask you to leave. Please pay for your meal and go." The bartender, a large man with suspenders and a handle-bar moustache, walked over and stood beside Max. "Now."

The angry woman grew very still and then she stood up and pushed the table away from her with such force that several glasses fell off and broke on the floor. "I will do no such thing." She picked up her keys and stormed out of the restaurant, bill unpaid.

Caro and the other woman with her stared straight ahead for a long moment before Caro bent down and began trying to pick up the glass shards.

"Please stop," Max said. "We will clean that up. Why don't

the two of you move to this table?" he pointed to a small one in the back corner of the restaurant, "and I'll bring you some chamomile tea."

Dad stood and followed Max toward the kitchen, and I made my way over to Caro and her friend. "Are you guys okay? That was pretty scary."

Caro nodded, even though I saw tears in her eyes. Her friend was sitting very still.

I tugged another chair over and sat down. "I'm Harvey," I said to the young woman I hadn't met yet.

She blinked a couple of times and then looked at me. "Sheila," she said as she forced a small smile onto her face. "I'm new to town."

"Sheila is our new Reiki master," Caro said. "She worked on Mayhem this morning."

I smiled at Caro and turned back to Sheila. "Is my girl a puddle like Caro promised?"

"Oh yes," Sheila said as some of the rigidness left her body. "She has some pretty sore back legs, but she will sleep soundly tonight." A soft smile made Sheila's dark brown skin glow like she was in a sunbeam.

"Oh, thank you," I said. "That girl played hard when she was a younger dog, and now that she's into middle-age, it's catching up to her."

"Well, feel free to bring her in regularly. It might just help her." Sheila took a deep breath. "I'm going to need to call my own practitioner after that." She glanced toward the door where the angry woman had just left.

No one had ever accused me of being too aloof about other people's business, so I didn't hesitate to ask. "What was that all about?"

Caro and Sheila exchanged a look and then Caro said, "That's our boss, Penelope. She isn't always, um, easy to work for."

"That's putting it mildly," Sheila said. "She's upset today because I'm giving free Reiki sessions."

I sighed. "Well, if it helps you, I'm happy to pay . . ." I wasn't exactly flush with cash, especially with the wedding coming up, but I didn't want Sheila to get in trouble for caring for my dog.

"Absolutely not," Caro said as Sheila nodded along. "Penelope knew we were giving first sessions for free when she suggested we bring in a Reiki practitioner. She doesn't get to go back on that decision just because she's running out of money."

I nodded but left that comment alone. As a business owner myself, I knew how hard it was, sometimes, to make ends meet, and while I didn't like how Penelope had talked to her employees, I wasn't going to judge the woman either, especially not about business finances.

"If she didn't own two Teslas and a Jaguar," Sheila said, "she'd have plenty of money."

I gaped but still stayed silent. People were always judging other people for what they spent money on. I saw it in the line when someone used government assistance to buy some soda for a birthday party and the person behind them thought they had a right to comment on the "use of their tax dollars." I wasn't about to do the same thing to someone in, maybe, a higher tax bracket than mine. Still, I did see Sheila's point.

"Well," I said as I stood up. "If it turns out that you need to skip Reiki for Taco, please do. No problem."

Sheila shook her head. "No, that guy has some serious tension built up in his hips. He needs me."

I smiled and went back to my table. "You heard her," I said to Dad, "Taco has tension in his hips." I tried to keep my face sincere.

"Sure he does," Dad said. "Let's get you back to work."

As we walked toward the door, I heard Max tell Caro and Sheila, "Your meal is paid for, women. Enjoy your day."

I glanced over at my dad, who didn't even smile.

. . .

I SPENT most of the afternoon wandering around the bookstore and talking to customers. Marcus was getting all our regularly weekly work taken care of with the help of Stephen and Walter, and now, apparently, Elle was at our house finishing up the landscaping with Pickle and Bear. Cate and Henrietta were completing the few remaining wedding-related tasks with Mom, and Dad had headed out to finalize a few "surprises" that Mom had come up with. While I was nervous about what my mother might add as a surprise for my life right now, I was immensely grateful for the mental space to just be in my store and talk books.

I had the privilege of suggesting two coffee table books, including the gorgeous collection of Frida Kahlo's complete paintings, to an art student who was graduating from nearby Washington College and had gotten a request for "exquisite" gift suggestions from her great aunt.

But by far, my favorite part of the afternoon was talking with two first graders who were excited to be able to pick out their favorite picture books since they had just gotten As in reading for the term. The three of us sat on the floor in the children's section and pulled book after book off the shelves as I told them why I loved the illustrations in one or the story in others. Their moms sat nearby and watched us with huge smiles on their faces.

Ultimately, they chose two titles a piece: *Knight Owl* by Christopher Denise, *The Little Ghost Who Was A Quilt* by Riel Nason, *The Night Gardener* by Terry and Eric Fan, and *Memory Jars* by Vera Brasgol. All of their choices were tender and sweet and beautifully illustrated, and the choice of two "night/knight" books gave me a chance to talk about homonyms, a subject the girls were still discussing as they headed out the door later.

By the time 5pm rolled around, and my shift at the store

was over, I felt sated in a way I hadn't in a long time because recently, I'd felt like I'd never quite done everything I needed to do in a day. Now, though, everything was finished – or at least getting done – and I had been both part of the doing and not responsible for it all. That was a great feeling.

After we bid goodbye to Marcus, Rocky and I walked out together. "See you tomorrow," she said and headed toward her car as I threw up a wave and made my way to the dog spa. When I got closer, I marveled at the adorable lights that framed the fire hydrant art out front and decided I'd ask Penelope if I could have the name of the artist so they could do something for my shop, too. Maybe we could make it a Main Street theme.

But all thoughts of art disappeared when I walked into the front door and found Caro and Sheila standing over Penelope's body, a pair of silver shears protruding from her chest.

2

For a very long moment, I stood, unmoving, as I stared at the scene, but then, I had my phone out and Jared on the line before I could even think. "Come to the dog spa. Now," I said before I hung up.

Caro and Sheila were still looking at Penelope's body. "Did you touch anything?" I said.

Both women finally noticed me and then both shook their heads. "No," Caro said. "I was in the back doing paperwork."

"And I was working with Taco," Sheila added as her face grew deathly white.

"You both need to sit down," I said as I walked over and took each of them by the arm to lead them to the small seating area by the window. "The police will be here in just a moment."

"The police?" Sheila asked quietly. "So she was murdered?" She stared at me intently, clearly waiting for an answer.

"I'd say the scissors sticking out of her chest are probably a pretty good indication of foul play," I replied in the sort of language I only used to hear on TV shows but was now part of typical dinner table conversation at my house.

"Someone stabbed her," Caro said as her eyes traveled back

to Penelope's body as her brain tried to make sense of what she was seeing.

The silence that settled around us was heavy, and after a minute or two, I realized it wasn't doing any of us any good to just sit there with the body. "Maybe we can go in the back, spend some time with the dogs."

Caro sprung to her feet. "The dogs." She was headed through the door behind the counter before I even processed what was happening, but then I hauled Sheila up to follow.

"Tell me about Taco," I said as I used my elbow to push up the door behind Caro.

Sheila stepped in front of me and then walked toward a room at the end of the hallway on the right. "He's just in here. Mayhem, too." She opened the door and walked in. There, Caro was sitting in the middle of the floor with a half-dozen dogs gathered round her, my two included.

"It's okay, pups," she was saying to them as she rubbed ears and scratched bellies. "It must feel scary in here just now, but you're okay. I'm calling your owners right now." She took out her phone and started to scroll.

"Actually, Caro, let's hold off on calling anyone, okay? Just until Jared, er, the police arrive." I knew – or at least I thought I knew - the impulse that was guiding the young woman. She wanted the animals safe and sound and away from this. But she obviously hadn't thought about the fact that those owners would be coming to get them would need to walk right by Penelope's body. "He and I can do doggy deliveries after he takes a look around."

I was sincere about shuttling the pups to their homes, but I also knew that Jared and the sheriff Tuck Mason would not want anyone else in here. . . and I expected they'd also want to check the dogs for evidence before they sent them on their way.

"Oh, okay?" Caro said as she slid her phone back in her

pocket as she looked up at me. "You know the officer who is coming?"

I flushed. "Yes, he's my fiancé," I said.

Caro frowned at me but then her face cleared. "We better feed them then." She looked up at Sheila.

"Okay," Sheila said and moved toward a big bin of kibble in the corner. "Who's hungry?" she said.

Four of the six canine heads turned in her direction, trained by their owners to know that second word. Mayhem and Taco were already walking her direction, and while I knew they could wait until we got home, I figured that the women needed something to do and that feeding the dogs wasn't going to destroy any evidence, at least I hoped not.

As the women set out six bowls and put a small amount of kibble in each one, I found a large metal bowl and filled it with water that I then set at the edge of the room, where it had less chance of being knocked over.

Just then, I heard the artificial bark that signaled the front door had opened, and I smiled when I heard Jared and Tuck's voices coming from the reception area. "Oh good, the police are here," I said as I took out my own phone and texted to tell Jared we were in the kennel with the dogs.

His reply was quick. "Stay put. Be back there in a minute."

"Tell me about these guys," I said as I glanced down at the dogs and then looked back up at the women. "I haven't met any of these other pooches before." I knew I was just filling the space with words, but we all needed less thinking and more filling just then.

"This here is Cyclops," Caro said as she scratched the ears of a black pug with, not surprisingly, only one eye. "He's ridiculous about tummy scratches." As if given the signal, Cyclops rolled over and exposed his belly.

Sheila was running her hand down the back of a chocolate brown dog a little bigger than Mayhem.

"Who's this?" I asked as I lowered myself to the floor beside her and rubbed another dog's belly.

"Carusoe," Sheila answered. "He's named after the opera singer. Chesapeake Bay Retriever."

"Does he sing?" I asked.

"Nope," Caro said with a small smile. "Doesn't even bark. He's deaf."

"Ah, so an ironic name," I get it.

The two women then introduced me to Cagney and Lacy, a pair of Jack Russell Terriers who, oddly enough, resembled their name sakes with one sporting a dark brown patch of fur on the top of his head and the other a ginger-orange one. "Their parents are big police drama fans, I take it," I said.

Sheila frowned. "Maybe." She looked very confused.

"Well, because they're named after the detectives on that TV show."

"What TV show?" Caro said.

"*Cagney and Lacy*. Those two women who were police officers in New York City."

Sheila and Caro just stared at me like I was speaking about some ancient Sumarian text that only three scholars had ever heard of instead of a very popular TV show from my childhood. Then, I thought of that meme that talked about how 1923 and 1973 were as far apart as 1973 from 2023, and I stopped talking. I might as well have been discussing Model Ts as the latest craze as far as these young women were concerned. Inwardly I groaned. Aging is not for the weak.

"Are their owners," I asked, "older . . . like me?"

"Oh yeah, pretty old. Wives. . . they just moved to town, the Dollins," Caro said.

"Haven't met them," I said. That was a surprise. St. Marin's was a very small town. "But I guess I will tonight."

Jared walked in. "I was going to say, if you were hiding puppies in here, Harvey Beckett," he turned to me with a small smile. He was trying to keep things light, but I could see the concern and strain in the set of his jaw.

"No puppies, but these six beauties are still pretty amazing." I introduced my fiancé to the four pups he didn't already know and then to Caro and Sheila, who didn't seem the least bit offended about getting second place after dogs. My dad would have been mortified, but we were all dog lovers here.

"Nice to meet you all," he said. "Caro, could Sheriff Mason and I talk to you in the hallway?"

Caro frowned but then nodded and stood to follow Jared out. He looked back at Sheila. "Please stay put we'd like to talk to you, too."

I knew it was standard procedure to talk to everyone from a crime scene separately, and I knew that Jared and Tuck would be direct but kind. And yet, the look of terror on Sheila's face made me wish we would all just sit here with the dogs and talk about what happened.

"Jared seems nice," she said without much enthusiasm. "This is horrible."

I sighed. "It is. Do you have someone you can call?" I had been in this situation more than once, and I was still shaken hard every time. It's so difficult to imagine a living person dead that actually seeing a dead body feels almost impossible, at least to me.

"My husband. Do you think it's okay if I call him now?" She looked near tears.

"I'm sure it is. Just don't tell him anything about what's happening, just that there's an emergency at work and he needs to come get you." I'd seen Jared and Tuck offer that same guidance in many situations.

She dialed and then said, "Hi. There's been a problem at work. Can you come get me in—" She looked over at me.

"Half an hour?" I said hoping that would be enough time for her to give her statement and be free to go.

"30 minutes," she said. "Yeah, I'm okay. See you soon." She paused. "I love you, too."

"Good," I said when she hung up. "Do you have any dogs?" This question brought a full smile to Sheila's face. "Six," she said.

"Six!" I nearly shouted. "Holy dog hair."

"You got that right. We vacuum every day." She laughed and started to tell me about the two Great Pyrenees, the two Saint Bernards, and the two rescue hounds they had. Her home sounded like absolutely gorgeous chaos.

"My two are enough for me," I said. "If I had six I would have surely broken my neck by now." Then told her about how Taco had a knack for laying right behind me when I was doing something so that when I stepped back I tripped over him and nearly fell. "Every day," I said.

Sheila laughed. "Well, when you have six, they move as a pack, and it's hard to keep that many dogs out of your line of sight." She chuckled. "The hardest part is when they all go to the bathroom with you."

Just the thought of six dogs in a bathroom had me laughing, and when Jared brought Caro back in and asked to talk with Sheila, she looked more relaxed than she had a few minutes ago.

Caro sat down and slid her leg under Caruso's head before she leaned down and put her forehead to his. "You like the big dogs, huh?" I said as I petted Mayhem and Taco, who had taken up their usual positions on either side of me.

She nodded. "The bigger the better."

"Sheila was just telling me she has four huge dogs. Have you met them?"

"Oh yeah," Caro chuckled. "I'm their dog sitter. That crew is a blast. All fur and slobber." She was smiling.

"You okay?" I said as I realized that she was crying even as she laughed.

She took a deep breath. "Not really, but I will be. It's just all, well, a lot."

It was a lot. "It is." Then I asked her the same question about calling someone that I had asked Sheila, and she gave her roommate a ring and asked her to come by. "She'll be here soon," Caro said.

For the next few minutes, the two of us sat quietly petting dogs and talking to them about how cute they were and how smart. Sometimes, the only creatures who really understood our feeling were our pets, I had learned, and it seemed like Caro needed their understanding more than mine right now.

Soon enough, Jared was back and saying that we could join them in the front of the shop. I had heard the woof alarm go off once a few minutes ago and had presumed that was the coroner, a fact that was confirmed when we stepped into the reception area and saw only a small smear of blood to indicate where Penelope's body had lain.

"Do you two have rides home?" Tuck said as the two women huddled together, three dogs on leashes for each of them.

"Yes," I said for them. "I suggested they call someone."

Tuck nodded. "Very good. Well, you two are free to go, but please do stay in town and available in case we need to ask you anything." His tone was friendly, but I knew the import in that statement. These women were suspects, and as such, Tuck needed to keep them close.

"I told Sheila and Caro that we'd take care of the dogs," I said to Jared, who winked and nodded.

"The shop will need to be closed for tomorrow," Tuck said as he walked the two women to the front door after they had handed Jared and me the leashes. "But you should be able to open the day after."

. . .

As Jared and I drove around with six dogs in his crew-cab pick-up, I decided I kind of like the wildness of the situation if not the cause of it. "This is kind of fun," I said as Cagney stood up and put her paws on Jared's shoulder like she was his navigator. Taco was laying on my feet in the wheel well, a little overwhelmed, it seemed.

"It is fun, but it's also a lot." He pushed Cagney back into the seat behind him. "I can't see if you stand on my shoulder, you goof."

Our drop-offs went smoothly, and we were able to explain that there had been a situation at the spa but that everything was under control. Fortunately, Jared was in plain clothes, so it didn't look like the police were escorting dogs to their owners. That might have raised a few more questions.

When we got home, Mayhem and Taco sped to the backyard, did their business, and then took to their respective beds, where they were snoring within seconds. Aslan, their crochety feline sister, took the snores as her signal to prance around the house like she was Fred Astaire, and while Jared and I made dinner, we had to keep shooing her off the counters, the one place in the house she was not allowed to go.

"Why does she do that?" Jared said. "I think she wants to be annoying on purpose."

"Oh, she definitely does. She has a brief window where she can be the center of attention, and she's not going to let the fact that we're cooking ruin her chance." I hefted the big girl off the counter one last time and then took out a roll of packing tape, which I used to make big loops of stickiness to add to the edge of the counter. It only took Aslan one attempt to learn that she didn't actually want to be on the counter. Apparently, tape was terrifying.

Instead, she tried to kill us by roping herself around our feet over and over again. She was nothing if not determined.

Finally, though, we got the table set with all our fixings,

sauces, and tortilla assortments and sat down to eat. Tacos had become a weekly staple in our house, but we had decided to make it a major event. So we took turns adding a "secret" ingredient to the menu each week, and both of us had to try it. Tonight was Jared's week, and he had decided he'd finally give avocado a try. I had been talking about the pleasure of guacamole on tacos since we met, but he had been unconvinced. I was glad to see him smile when he took his first bite.

"See, I told you," I said, a self-appointed expert in the food since I had lived in California for a few years. "The creaminess is really nice, isn't it?"

"Actually, yeah, but I was thinking it was more about how it cuts the heat of the habanero sauce really well."

I nodded as I shoved most of a taco into my mouth. "That's why Lu has it as a staple for most of her dishes." Lu was our friend, and the sheriff's wife, who ran a Mexican food truck that served, hands-down, the best tacos I'd ever eaten. But since we'd been trying to save money for the wedding and our eventual honeymoon, we hadn't eaten her tacos in a while. I missed them and said so.

"Well, just a few days, and you'll get all of Lu's food that you want," Jared said as he fixed another taco for himself, with avocado.

"That's going to be the highlight of the day," I said deadpan and then looked at my fiancé out of the corner of my eye, where I found his mouth open as he stared at me.

"The highlight of our wedding day is going to be the food, huh?" He shook his head. "I was going to say it was going to be the flowers, but alright."

We both laughed as we continued to eat. But then, I said, "This murder, though ... "

"It's not going to interrupt our wedding, Harvey," Jared said and kissed my cheek, smearing a small bit of avocado beneath my eye.

"No, I wasn't worried about that," I said honestly as I wiped away from the food. "I just hate that someone died in our town this week. Kind of dampens the mood, you know?" I felt kind of selfish saying that, but it was true. I had been hoping that our wedding week would be beyond perfect.

But this was St. Marin's, and I was me. I should have learned to anticipate that a murder might happen near me at any moment.

Jared took my hand. "Yeah, but you know, maybe this is a good thing."

I raised an eyebrow.

"I mean, not a good thing in the sense that a woman was killed." He pulled his hand down his face. "I just mean it gives you something else to focus on instead of worrying about the wedding."

I smiled. "That is true, and now that Mom has taken over the organizing, I can actually look into the murder."

Jared shook his head and held up one hand. "What? Your mother is now organizing?"

I sighed. "She and everyone else. Apparently, Rocky thought I looked overextended, so she brought in the team. Everyone has their marching orders."

"I don't," Jared said.

"Me neither, but I bet if we ask Mom, she'll say our only job is to show up in the right clothes on Sunday." I smiled at him and let out a long sigh. "Actually, it is kind of a relief."

"You are glad to have the help then?" My fiancé knew me, and he knew that accepting help was really, really hard for me. As a kid, I had come to understand accepting help, even when it was offered, was burdening someone else with my problems. I was only now unlearning the trauma response of radical self-sufficiency.

"I am," I said before letting my face open into a wide grin. "Besides now I can get to sleuthing."

Jared looked at me and smiled. "I already talked to Tuck, and while neither of us thrilled to have you getting yourself into potential danger – AGAIN – we know it's better to work with you than to try to convince you not to do anything and have you hide what you are doing."

"I'm so glad you're learning," I said as I leaned over to kiss him on the cheek. He wasn't wrong. Tuck had tried to stop my sleuthing when I had first moved to St. Marin's, but despite my best efforts – and I really had tried – I just couldn't keep my curiosity at bay. It really was better all around if they just looped me in. "I'll get started tomorrow. I think Mayhem may need more Reiki."

"Just remember it'll have to be a house call. We're keeping the spa closed another day so we can do a final sweep for evidence," Jared said as he cleared our plates from the table.

"Even better," I said. The wheels of my mind were already turning.

SHEILA RESPONDED ENTHUSIASTICALLY when I called her the next morning to ask if she'd mind coming to our place to treat Mayhem again. "She really did seem to be better," I said, and I meant it. This morning, the hound hadn't stretched for a full ten minutes just to get moving. She was actually a little bouncy.

And at 10am when the doorbell rang and the pup caught the scent of the woman who was, apparently, her new best friend, she began to hop around in excitement. "Someone is very glad you're here," I said as I greeted Sheila.

"That makes two of us." She bent down and scratched Mayhem behind her ears before noticing that Taco was looking forlorn nearby. As she walked over to greet him, she said, "Maybe I can do a two-for-one special today. This guy just needs the loving, I think."

I smiled. "That would be great, but don't let him fool you. That's just his resting basset face."

Sheila cackled as she scanned the room. "I think the middle of the living room floor is our best space," she said, "if you don't mind."

"Not at all," I said and shifted the coffee table out from in front of the couch. "Do you need anything else? Towels? Hot water?"

She laughed again. "We're not delivering a baby, Harvey. I really just could use a glass of water for myself."

"Water I can do." As I headed into the kitchen to grab her drink, I heard her coaxing Mayhem over with whispers and clicks, and by the time I got back to the trio, Mayhem was fully laid out on her side, eyes half-closed as Sheila's hands lingered over her back legs.

"Poor girl. She hurt herself a long time ago?"

I studied my graying pup as she started to snore. "Yeah, when she was really young, she ran very hard and, the vet thinks, tore some ligaments in her back legs. It hasn't slowed her down much except for jumping."

Sheila nodded as she closed her eyes and continued to move her hands a couple of inches above Mayhem's body. I took a seat on the couch and pretended to read a book, *The Kiss Curse*, while I watched her work. I still wasn't sure what I thought about reiki in general, but maybe my opinion didn't matter because Mayhem was loving it.

When Sheila took a break before working on Taco, I asked her if she wanted a cup of tea and invited her into the kitchen while I brewed some for us. "How are you?" I asked as she took a seat on one of the stools by the peninsula.

She sighed and folded her arms across her chest. "I'm okay, I guess. It was all just such a shock."

I nodded. I had been exactly where she was far too many

times, and still, it was always a shock. "Any word on when services will be held?"

"No, not yet. Penelope has—had a son, so I expect he's taking care of everything. But we haven't heard a word." She took the blue and white mug from my hands and held it close to her chest. "I can't imagine there will be a lot of guests, though," she said and then looked up at me quickly. "Sorry, that was cruel."

I shook my head and waved a hand in front of my face. I had to look casual or I wasn't going to get much information. "Why do you say that?"

Sheila took a sip of her tea and then leaned back. "I don't want to speak ill of the dead." She paused, but then spoke anyway, as we all do when we invoke that phrase. "You saw how she was in the restaurant. She was just a volatile person. Very prone to anger."

"Yeah, that was pretty intense. She did that a lot?" I asked.

"No, not a lot, but sometimes, she'd just fly into a rage over the smallest thing. And she wasn't very forthcoming about her own life, so it was hard to overlook those rages." She met my eyes. "You know, you can give people a lot of grace if you know you're going through something."

I took a long sip of my own chamomile. "Yeah, I get that. It's much easier to take it personally when you don't know the 'behind the scenes,' so to speak." In my own life, I tried to remember that adage about how we never know the whole story of anyone's life and so we need to give grace. But that would be hard to do in the face of such abusive treatment.

"Exactly," Sheila said as she stood and set her mug in the sink. "If she treated everyone like she treated Caro and me, then well..."

She didn't have to finish her sentence. I knew just what she meant. If she was that volatile with everyone, then we had a load of suspects to consider.

3

"You know," Mart said when I called her after Sophie left, "I think people in St. Marin's are usually sort of sickly nice. You know, almost too caring to be real, as if they have an agenda?"

"Except they don't," I added.

"Exactly," she said. "It's like that guy from college who was fit, handsome, smart, and also kind – you want to hate him but you can't because he's such a good person. That's how I feel about almost everyone in our town."

I knew just what she meant. People here went above and beyond to love on one another. The usual Southern casseroles when there's tragedy, but also tiny gifts left at the door for no reason than some anonymous person in town thought of you when they saw it. It was almost too good to be true.

"All I'm saying," Mart continued, "is that I keep being surprised by the number of real jerks that live in our town. How have I not run into them before they are killed?"

I chuckled and then immediately regretted it. Death was no laughing matter, even if the person who had died was a real, um, meanie. "I think people that really struggle with good behavior, well, maybe they just keep to themselves."

"Or they pick the people who have so little power that they can't really do anything about how they're being treated," she added.

"That, too," I said, "but in this case, surely more people than just her employees knew that Penelope, um, struggled with kindness."

"Oh, the euphemisms you come up with to try and avoid saying unkind things, Harvey. You are a natural for this town." She sighed. "But you're right. Maybe the customers?"

That was a good idea. I expected that Penelope held it together for most people, but if she was a volatile as I'd seen her be the day before, then she had probably lost her cool with at least a few customers. "I'll asked Sophie and Caro for ideas."

Mart cleared her throat. "Is that a good idea, Harv?"

I paused. "Why? They'd know."

"Yes, they would, but they are also suspects."

My heart panged with that dose of reality, but she was right. "So they might exaggerate or fabricate—"

"Exactly. Is there another way?" In the background, I heard a muffled group of voices. "Think about it. I've got to go. Our tasters are here."

I laughed. "Pour away," I said as I hung up. Mart still worked a few shifts in the tasting room at the winery even though she was mostly marketing and sales now. She said it kept her in touch with the customer base, and I totally understood. I couldn't imagine not working the floor of my shop. I just loved seeing people find books they got excited about, and while I could now afford to hire more staff and mostly oversee things from afar, I didn't want to.

Now, though, I had a more pressing problem. Mart was right that the customers had probably felt Penelope's wrath from time to time, so I just had to figure out a way to identify them. I pondered my methods as the dogs and I walked to the store to begin my afternoon shift.

"Where do I learn about customer complaints for my store?" I asked myself outloud as Mayhem and Taco gave a shrub at the corner a full sniff-down. Sometimes, rarely though, someone complained in person, but mostly, I heard about dissatisfaction through online reviews.

"That's it," I said as I punched my fist into the air, startling the two dogs whose leashes were attached to that hand. I pulled my phone out and opened the review app that I tried not to scan obsessively. A quick search for Penelope's spa led me right to what I was looking for.

"I have never been treated more cruelly by a store owner than I was today. I won't repeat the language she used to me and about my dog because I have manners, but let's just say, I won't be visiting her establishment again." – Riki F.

Whew, well, that was one. And as I read, with the exception of a few glowing reviews spattered amongst the negative ones, the pet spa had been lambasted with complaints, tyrades, and even threats to take Penelope to the Better Business Bureau.

Of course, the people most likely to write reviews were the ones with a bee in their bonnets – I knew that. But still, the consistency of the critiques here was telling – they were almost all about poor treatment from the spa owner to both the humans and their pets. No one complained about the grooming or treatments, just about the abusive attitude of that "tall blonde hun of a woman", as one reviewer called her.

I winced as I finished up scanning through the reviews for the last year. Clearly, Penelope had some struggles, and she was taking them out on her customers. If she was scaring off business like this, I could see why she didn't want to give anything away free reiki – she had to be in dire straits cash-wise.

Between customers that afternoon, I pondered how to identify the reviewers from the site. Most used handles or just first names and initials, and I didn't think that clicking on their profiles was going to give me direct contact information. This was a dilemma.

Fortunately, one of my favorite customers, Galen Gilbert came in with his adorable and aged bulldog Mack. The two of them were walking a bit more slowly these days, and the gray on their heads was becoming more pronounced. But they still read more than any pair I knew – okay, Mac didn't read, but he still had exquisite taste, as demonstrated by the fact that he lured Taco and Mayhem off their beds by pretending like he was going to play a game of tag before promptly taking the ortho-pedic bed that Mayhem had been laying on. He was no dummy.

I gave my friend a hug as we laughed at the bulldog's wizened ways, and then I said, "He's a sneaky one."

"You don't have to tell me. I have to ply him with bacon just so I can get into bed first at night," Galen said with a laugh, and I was suddenly flooded with the image of the old man racing to his bed and his dog gulped down strips of bacon.

"Oh my. Someone has someone well-trained," I said.

"You know it?" Galen said with a smile. "Wouldn't have it any other way."

Me neither, I thought. "What are you looking for today? More cozies?"

"Always," Galen said. "But I want to go into the paranormal ones. Recommendations?"

As one of the few men I knew who read cozy mysteries, Galen had a very discerning eye when it came to his books of choice. He didn't want any weak women or heroic men. The things he enjoyed most were women saving themselves and rich, complex friendships. I couldn't blame him. I read cozies for the same reason.

"Alrighty then," I said as we walked toward the mystery section. "Witches okay?"

"More than okay," he said.

I began pulling books off the shelf, anticipating that Galen would, as usual, buy a dozen or so. Soon, his arm was loaded with Scarlett Moss's *This Book Was Made For Spellin'*, *Haunted Hunches* by Rosie A. Point and Allie Katt, *Boardwalk Betrayal* by Wendy Ledger, and a bunch more titles. "You're going to be magic-ed out," I said as I helped him carry his books to the register.

"I doubt it," he said. "My new Substack is all about cozies, and I want to read thematically by month."

"Ooh, that's fun. Do you have your theme for next month chosen?"

He grinned. "Of course. 19th century historical."

I jotted that down on the notebook I kept by the register just for customer recommendations. "I'll get some more of those in."

"Thanks," he said as I rang up his purchase with the friends and family discount. "Do you want to leave Mack here?" The bulldog often spent a leisurely afternoon snoozing with his friends while Galen ran other errands.

"Not today," he said. "He's got an appointment at the pet spa."

I grimaced. "Actually, they're closed today. Didn't someone call you?"

Galen shook his head. "No, everything okay?"

I quickly and quietly told Galen about the murder, and then it occurred to me that he might have a solution for my reviewer dilemma. I explained what I was doing, and he immediately had an answer.

"Ask your fiancé," he said with a wink.

I rolled my eyes. "Well, obviously I could do that, but I'm trying to find this out on my own."

A twinkle bounced into Galen's eye. "I'm afraid he's a bit

ahead of you on this one, Harvey. He called me this morning with the same question."

I groaned. Of course Jared had called him. Galen was the most social media savvy person we knew, and if anyone had a way to track down reveiwers, it would be him.

"Any chance you want to tell me what you told him?" I said sweetly.

"Not a bit," he said. "I don't interfere with police work." He held my gaze, intent on imparting his silent advice.

"Fair," I said. "And thanks for the tip."

He sighed and tucked his tote bag under his shoulder. "Well, since Mack won't be getting his spa day, would you mind if he stayed here for a bit? I'll come back and get him before dark."

"Sounds great," I said as I gazed over at the three dogs snoozing in the window and snoring so loudly that customers were giggling with delight. "I may have to charge you for drool removal, though."

"That's only fair," he said and headed out the door.

As I WANDERED the store and watched Marcus recommend the Eerie Elementary series to a kid who looked to be about six – "The school comes alive," Marcus said much to the child's delight – I conceded what I probably should have realized already: I wasn't going to be able to do this on my own.

I took out my phone, tapped out a text to Jared, and let myself settle into the idea of a partnership in this investigation. After all, I was entering into a lifelong one with this man this very weekend. Might as well acquiesce to the fact that sometimes I needed – even wanted – help, especially from someone who respected me, knew I could do most things myself, and never, ever condescended to me.

By the time Jared texted back a few minutes later, I was

actually kind of excited about delving into this with him. And his reply cinched that for me. "Be there in 15. I've got the list."

When Jared arrived, we set up a work station in the café so that I could keep an eye on the floor and help Marcus out when needed. And so I could caffeinate regularly. Normally by mid-afternoon I was off caffeine for the day, but the week of my wedding when there was a murder seemed like a reasonable to time let that rule slide.

Rocky raised an eyebrow when I asked for a regular vanilla latte and said, "How about half-caf?"

I sighed. "Okay, if you think that's necessary."

"It's absolutely necessary," she said. "We cannot have a sleep deprived bride on Saturday."

She did have a point, so I carried my half-strength latte to the table and sat down across from my fiancé. "What have we got?" I said as I pulled the warm mug to my mouth.

I could almost see Jared restraining himself from an eye roll at the word "we," but he didn't hesitate. "Well, I narrowed down the complaintants to four."

I nodded. "What criteria did you use to eliminate the others?" I glanced down at the app on my phone and quickly counted at least 15 vitriolic reviews.

"Well, I figured that for someone to get worked up enough to kill someone the situation had to be pretty extreme for them," Jared said as he ran his eyes over his notebook and then spun it so I could read it.

"These folks," he said as he tapped his index finger over a few names he'd crossed out, "posted similar reviews for a bunch of different companies."

"So they're probably just angry people, not people with a particular grudge against Penelope or her spa."

"Exactly," Jared said with a smile. "So when I eliminated the grumpy, perpetual complainers," he glanced around as if someone might have overheard him and then continued, "I was left with these four."

On the page, I saw four of the screennames from the reviews, and beside them, Jared had jotted what I assumed were legal first and last names. "Trevor Ball, Grady Cleaver, Mecklenburg Veluz, and Dior Stephens."

"Alright, then, so what do we know about these folks?" I said as I jotted the names into the notes app on my phone.

"Well, I hadn't gotten that far yet, so want to take two and I'll take two?" His grin almost reached his ears when he asked.

"You have to ask?" I said with my own smile. "I'll take Trevor Ball and Mecklenburg Veluz."

"You just took Mecklenburg because you know it'll be easy to find information," he said.

"You know it, but you have Dior Stephens and Grady Cleaver – surely those won't be too hard." I inwardly groaned because Trevor Ball was not going to be that simple to track down, I expected.

"True," Jared said as he took his phone out of his front pocket and frowned at the screen. "I have to get back to the station, but maybe we can continue this tonight at home."

"Everything okay?" I so wanted to pry, but there were limits to how much my fiancé and the sheriff let me get involved in police business.

"I'm not sure," Jared said as he stood up and carried our mugs to the counter. "I hope so."

I walked him to the door and then he kissed my cheek. "See you at home."

Just the idea of the fact that we shared a home together made me all warm and gooey inside.

For the next few hours, as I rang up customers and helped the most stylish older woman pick out a baking book for her new boyfriend – she chose *Anna Olson's Baking Wisdom*, a lovely collection of recipes and tips that I thought her boyfriend would love – I began looking for my two suspects. I started with Trevor Ball first, mostly because I thought he would take the most work.

Surprisingly, though, it turned out there was only one Trevor Ball on the Eastern Shore, and he lived in Easton. I quickly found his address and texted it over to Jared with the note, "1-0."

He sent back an eye-rolling emoji that made me laugh.

I was certain Jared would want to go talk to everyone on the list, but I thought maybe we could find out a bit more about these people and have some more clarity before we rolled up on their houses.

So I took to social media, and with his town and name, I was able to find Trevor Ball, a rather unassuming (from his pictures) middle-aged man with a combover that was, surprisingly, effective, and a very good sense of taste in shoes. His feed seemed pretty normal – pictures of his children and wife, a few of him golfing, a rather remarkably fondness for his Maine Coon cat. All in all, he seemed like a pretty typical, white, straight American guy.

Next, I went to Google, and quickly saw what had raised Jared's antennae about Mr. Trevor Ball. His handle – TrevMan06 – was all over reviews for retailers, restaurants, and even the school his children attended. And every review was full of capital letters, expletives, and demands for full refunds. I read about a dozen of his comments, and I felt all tingly and icky, like someone had insulted me personally. This dude had some issues for sure.

As I was about to begin looking for Mecklenburg Veluz, the bell over the front door of the store rang, and my friend Cate came in, carrying a large canvas that looked like it weighed more than she did, a feat which would not have been hard since Cate weighed less than the bags of dogfood I bought in bulk.

"Is that it?" I said as I walked over and took the edge of the canvas to help her carry it.

"This is it," she said and led me over to the front of the counter, where we leaned the mixed media piece against it. "What do you think?"

I stared at this newest piece of art for the shop, and my throat tightened. "It's amazing," I said with a rasp. "She did an incredible job."

The piece showed stacks of books on a small, round table beside a purple velvet armchair just like the one I had added recently to the fiction section of the store. The pages of the books were practically flipping in the air, and the way the artist had captured the light from the antique iron lamp that stood behind the chair was magical. "It looks so real."

"It looks like your store, Harvey, and your heart, too," Cate said as she squeezed my shoulders. "Where do you want it?"

For a moment, I thought about hanging it right there on the front of the register so it would get the attention it deserved, but I quickly thought better of that given all the knees and tiny hands that rubbed against that counter every day. "How about we hang it by the stage?" I suggested instead.

The small reading area we'd added a couple years back had become a favorite hangout place for teenagers after school, Moms with wine on weekend evenings, and even a fly fishing group that used it as a fly-tying school a couple times a month. So I knew the art would get a lot of focus here, but it would also be out of the way and safe from tiny, sticky hands. I could handle my books getting marred by jam and candy from small children, but this piece was one of a kind. It had to be protected.

"I hope it's okay," Cate said as we stepped back and looked at the piece, "but I told the artist she could come by and see it later today."

"Oh, that's more than okay," I said. "Do you know when

she's coming? I'd love to do a little presentation when she's here."

Cate glanced down at her watch. "Actually, I think she may be on her way over now. She was closing up her studio when I left, and I think she was going to stop by before she headed home."

"Amazing," I said. I took a deep breath and looked at my friend. "Forgive me, but with all that's going on, I've forgotten her name. Remind me?"

"Oh, she paints as Toggle," Cate said with a smile as she pointed at the signature on the bottom of the canvas.

I shook my head. "That's right. Of course."

"But her real name is Mecklenburg. Everybody calls her Meck." Cate smiled. "You'll really like her."

I sighed. "I hope so." My heart was jumping in my chest because, of course, the woman who had made one of the most beautiful pieces of art I'd ever seen and made it just for me was a suspect in the murder that my fiancé and I were investigating. Of course. This is how my life worked, and I could either rail against it or trust the universe that all the intersections were meaningful.

Cate studied my face. "What's wrong?"

"Nothing," I said with a deep sigh. "Let's make an announcement over the PA about the new piece, see if we can gather people for when she arrives." Might as well make the best of this wild situation.

After I filled Marcus in and heard his announcement about the new art piece, I waited for Jared by the back door. He'd responded immediately, of course, to my text that said Mecklenberg Veluz coming to the store shortly. "Do not say anything about Penelope or the murder. Be there in five." His text was in all caps, and even though we were old, we were young enough to know that all caps was the equivalent of shouting. I heard him and had no intention of being along with anyone who might have killed anyone, ever.

Still, I was getting antsy as first five, then six, then seven minutes passed, and he wasn't here yet. Cate was hanging in the café with Rocky as she waited for Toggle to arrive, and I had this sinking feeling that the artist was going to beat Jared here. I was gripping my phone so hard that my thumb was starting to ache.

But just when I was about to panic text Jared, I heard the bell over the front door and looked over to see Tuck coming in with another deputy close behind him. At that same moment, I heard a key in the back door, and Jared stepped in.

My panic must have shown on my face because Jared quickly took my hand and pulled me into the storage room, where he hugged me close. "It's okay, Harvey. We're here. We've got the situation under control."

I felt the tightness in my chest ease a bit, but that bit of relief only made me understand how very anxious I had been. In fact, my breath was still ragged, and I couldn't see quite straight.

"Sit down, Harvey," Jared said, pulling one of the folding chairs out from under the table in the corner. "Put your head between your knees and breath in for five then out for six. Focus on your breathing."

I did as he instructed and felt my heart rate slow just a bit. I started to lift my head, but Jared put gentle pressure on my neck. "Stay there for ten minutes. Just breathe." His left thigh pressed against my shoulder as he shifted a bit in his stance.

A moment later, Rocky was sitting cross-legged on the floor beside me, and I heard the door open and close behind Jared. "He's going to talk with the artist," she said as she stroked her hand up and down my shin. "Keep breathing."

I sighed and let my breath come a bit more slowly still.

"How is that all of you know how to manage a panic attack when I, tqhe one having one, have no idea?"

Rocky chuckled. "If the situations were reversed, you'd do the same thing. It's just natural to help someone you love return to calm. No special trick there, just doing what feels right."

I nodded a little. "Tell me about what you're reading?" Nothing soothed me more than thinking about books, and while I couldn't draw up much about my own reading currently, as Rocky began to speak, the wild fury of thought that had been flowing behind my eyes slowed.

"Well, I just started my second TJ Klune book. I loved *The House in the Cerulean Sea,* and so far, I'm really liking *Under the Whispering Door.*"

I didn't say anything, just let her words sink into me.

"They're kind of like Frederick Bachman meets that Miss Peregrine's guy. Magic kids. Grumpy men who, it turns out, are just really sad and lonely. But also queer and rich with fantasy." She paused for breath. "You'd like them," she said.

I slowly sat back and sighed. "I think I would. I"ll add them to my list." I took one more very deep breath and said, "Thank you, Rocky."

She smiled. "If only all our emotional challenges were solved by books."

"Aren't they?" I asked with a smile as we both got slowly to our feet. "Clearly, though, I need a bit more than books to help me with my stuff, huh?"

Rocky tucked her arm around my shoulders. "Want me to recommend someone?"

I nodded. "Yeah, it's time." Once again, I sighed and then headed for the door. "But first, let's meet our suspect, I mean artist."

Rocky squeezed me and then held the door open. "After you, Boss," she said.

I rolled my eyes. She and Marcus were far more than my employees, as I'd told them many times, but they did really seem to enjoy calling me "boss." Maybe I'd suggest they do it in different languages so we all built our vocabulary a bit.

That thought brought a small smile to my face as I approached Jared, who was facing me while talking to a slight, dark-haired woman with her back to me.

I walked over and stood next to Jared. "You must be Toggle," I said. "I love the painting." I smiled up at the art hanging to our left. "It's perfect for the store."

The young woman returned my smile and then said, "I'm so glad you like it. I always find it an art in itself to balance my style with the client's request. Yours was a special challenge."

She took a step closer to the painting, and I stepped up beside her. "How so?"

"Well," she said as her face seemed to shine with delight, "I knew words were important. It's a bookstore after all, but I'm Filipino. So I didn't want only English words." She pointed to the spines of the books. "So I put in some Tagalog words, too."

I leaned closer and read the text in tiny print out loud. "Vocabulary. Syntax." I pointed to the third book in the stack. "That one's in Tagalog?"

Toggle smiled. "Yes, *aklat* means book."

I loved that and grinned. "And the other words in Tagalog?" I asked as I noticed two more.

"*Pahina* is page, and *salita* is word or language." She sighed. "Pretty basic, but I thought it fit with the others."

I nodded. "Absolutely. It's a tiny detail, but I love that they're all word words." I turned back to her and grinned. "Thank you again. I have the check for you at the register whenever you're heading out." I glanced quickly at Jared. "Oh goodness, I just realized I may have been interrupting. Sorry. I got carried away."

Jared smiled. "It's hard not to when it comes to art with you,

Harv," he said. "But yeah, Ms. Veluz and I need to chat a bit more if you don't mind."

I furrowed my brow in an attempt to look puzzled and then said, "My store is your store." Then I winked at Toggle. "How do you say that in Tagalog?"

"Ang iyong tindahan ay ang aking tindahan," she said with a grin. "I'll give you lessons if you'd like."

"Oh, I'd very much like." And as I said it, I decided I was being honest. I liked this woman, which was going to be a shame if she turned out to be a murderer.

Toggle and Jared headed toward the café, and I made my way back to the register to get our the artist's check and give Marcus an update. If there was one thing I'd learned in all these murder-y situations over the past few years, it's that my friends were the only thing keeping me from going entirely over the edge into constant panic. They needed to be up to speed.

JARED OBVIOUSLY FELT the same way because when he finished his talk with Toggle, who I gladly paid because even if she was a murderer the painting was perfect and I paid artists for their work, he sent a text to our friend group. "Potluck tonight. All Booked Up. Theme – Thai."

We'd been having these informal gatherings at my store ever since I opened it. Everyone brought something around our central theme, and my mom coordinating the meal so that we didn't, again, end up with six macaroni and cheeses. No one had complained, but our hearts appreciated at least a little bit more ruffage and vitamin content typically.

So at 7pm, when we closed the store down, the bell kept ringing as our friends piled in with everything from pad thai to spring rolls to Stephen and Walter even brought pitchers of thai iced tea and one of Sabai Sabai, a mixed drink that had, apparently, a Thai whiskey in it with lime juice. Given my earlier bit of mental unbalance, I opted for the non-alcoholic option, which was delicious.

But I did fill up on drunken noodles, my favorite Thai dish, which Jared had ordered for me "medium spicy" so that I could enjoy the burn and still manage to eat my food. My experienment with "Thai spicy" had not gone well last time. By the time, we were all seated with our plates, I finally felt back to normal, if strangely exhausted from my earlier panic attack.

"So we're here to figure out who killed Penelope Fisker, right?" Cate asked as she lifted one of her husband's pan-fried Roti toward her mouth.

Tuck guffawed. "I'm fairly sure that Jared and I have that actual investigation under control, thank you very much," he said as he patted the corners of his mouth exaggeratedly with his napkin.

"We do," Jared agreed, "but we do need your help with something. Does anyone here know Celestial Veluz"

Tuck's wife Lu coughed. "The person's name mean *heavenly light*?" she asked once she got her air back. "Really?"

Jared let a small smile play across his lips. "Apparently. Apparently, the Veluz family has a flourish for names."

"So she's related to Mecklenburg?" Marcus asked.

"Yes, her mother," Jared said. "And from what I gather from Mecklenberg, I mean Toggle – she prefers that – her mother had some very strong feelings about our resident dog spa owner."

I sat forward. "Tell me more."

Mart shot me a look and put her hand on my knee. "Whoa, girl. You're sitting this one out."

I looked over at her. "I most certainly am not," I said even as I heard the alarming squeak in my voice. "I'm not sitting out."

"Yes, Harvey, you are," Tuck said as he scooted to the edge

of his folding chair. "We can handle this. You need to take care of yourself."

My mother leaned over from where she sat on the other side of Mart and put her hand on top of Mart's. "Yes, you do. Let us handle this."

Jared cleared his throat. "The police are handling this," he said with a firm look at my mother, a look that seemed to communicate more than a simple reassertion of responsibility. "But if any of you know Ms. Veluz, could you let me know? I need to ask for your help."

With that, Jared settled back with his knee against mine and began to eat the impressive plate of food he had assembled for himself. I looked at him carefully. "That's it. No further discussion."

"Nope," my mom said. "The police have got it, as Jared said, and we have more important things to do." Her eyes twinkled as she stood up. "Who is ready for a shower?"

It took me a minute to realize my mother was not suggesting some strange group bonding experience and, instead, was handing out party hats before slipping a sash that said "Bride To Be" over my head while Dad gave Jared a matching one for the groom.

"You didn't think we were going to let this thing happen without a party, did you?" Mart said as she slid her phone out of her pocket and took the Bluetooth speaker that Henri handed her.

"Well, no," I said as my mind tried to catch up. "I *thought* the party was going to happen on Saturday."

"Oh, we're partying then, too, girl," my friend Elle said as she walked over and pulled me to my feet. "This is just the pre-game."

I squinted at my farmer friend. "What do you know about pre-game?"

"Woman, I have tailgated enough Ravens' games to know

how to party before the real party gets going." Then Elle turned to Mart and said, "Turn it up."

Let's just be clear. I am not a partyer. I would much rather have a dinner party with six good friends or sit in a room reading with those same six people than try to figure out how to dance or stay standing after consuming one too many glasses of champagne.

But there's something kind of magical about a party with the people you love most in the world. The way you can be yourself and not worry about being judged or teased, it's really freeing. These people know the best and worst of you and love you for it all.

So that night, I let loose. Now, I wasn't going to be on some new reality show about middle-aged women partying, but I did drink a bit more than I normally would and I danced, as they say, like no one was watching. It was a great night, and while I might not have been the best judge of everyone else's enjoyment, it did seem like they had a good time.

At least, for a bit, we all forgot about the murder.

4

Our collective amnesia about Penelope's death and the potential that an artist we loved had killed her was short-lived, however, when a reporter from the Easton paper showed up to interview me about our newest acquisition for the store.

Normally, we'd have put a press release out about the new addition, and so on a typical day I would have been thrilled to get the media attention. But given the situation, I found myself standing tongue-tied and dry-mouthed by the painting while a very nice young woman – who looked to be about 13 – asked me questions.

She wasn't probing with deep questions or working an angle – it was clear this was going to be a lifestyle piece, not a revelatory article of investigative journalism. And yet, I found myself overthinking everything I said about the reason I had bought the art, the symbolism of the books, and even the artist herself because I was so afraid I was going to slip and say something about how she was a suspect in St. Marin's latest murder.

Not for the first time, Marcus saved me by coming over to talk about how the piece reflected the general aesthetic and mission of the store – a deep love for books and a desire to give as many people access to them as possible.

"Like a library," the reporter said as she made a note in her very official look steno book.

Something about that expression snapped me back into focus. "Yes," I said, "although we could never want to take the place of our local libraries. They are heart and soul and safety of a community." I took a deep breath and tried to put into words something I had been thinking for a long time. "We are the public space that allows you to curate your own library. Here, you can come, browse, explore, taste, and then take home what you want to have near you forever. We want to be the place you build your book collection wisely."

Marcus grinned at me as the reporter scribbled furiously and then looked up with a smile. "So this piece by Toggle, it's meant to show the way your store intersects with people's homes via the books?"

For a brief moment I just looked at this bright-eyed young woman, and then I smiled. "Yes, that's it exactly."

We exchanged a bit more information, and I assured her that she was welcome to contact me via email if she had any more questions, and she left.

Then, I took myself to the backroom and cried just a little, again. The reporter had captured exactly why I loved that painting and now, I couldn't enjoy it hardly at all because it was possible the artist had killed a person.

"But *possible* is the thing here, Harvey?" I said to myself as I wiped my eyes. "It's only possible that Toggle did this. And if she didn't, you deserve to enjoy her painting with abandon." I stood up straight and took a deep breath. "Time to solve a murder," I said quietly as I went back onto the floor.

Since it appeared that Marcus had the register covered, I made my way to the pets and animals section, hoping that maybe a good alphabetizing session with lots of creatures might spark something in my mind. So I set myself down on the floor and began with the "Cagey Critters" as I had dubbed the section dedicated to hamsters, gerbils, guinea pigs, chinchillas, and anything else that lived in a cage.

Inspiration about the murder did not strike as I slid *All Things Guinea Pigs For Kids* into place, but I did have the idea to consolidate the shelves in this case and do a guinea-pig picture book display at the top. We had some great titles, and as I went to get retrieve *The Three Little Guinea Pigs, The Adventures Of Marshmellow,* and other titles, a twinkle of an idea came to mind. Maybe we needed to look wider than customers of Penelope's pet spa. Maybe we needed to consider her competitors. Maybe even her colleagues.

As I set each of the display titles on the top shelf, being sure to angle them so parents could see the titles when they came to get their children, or themselves, guinea pig handbooks, I began to make a mental list of other business owners who might have worked with Penelope. We didn't have any other pet spas in town, but we did have two vets, a pet store, and a traveling dog groomer. Maybe they'd have something to add to what we knew.

With the display set and a text request sent to Cate to ask her to please draw a guinea pig on card stock for me, I stepped outside for a bit of fresh spring air and called Jared. I didn't even say hello when he answered and began, instead, with the charming opening of "We need to talk to animal people."

"Hi Harvey. How is your day?" He said, and I could hear the laughter in his voice. "Fine, Jared," he added, making his voice slightly higher and far more sing-songy than mine. "Just selling books and drinking coffee. How about yours?"

I chuckled. "Alright, how is your day going?" I said, feeling the urgency that I now realized was part of my newly-diagnosed ADHD, threatening to make me terse or cold and repressing that possibility. "Things okay?"

My fiancé laughed. "Things are more than okay. I'm marrying you this week. How could they not be bad?" He let that statement settle into the airwaves between us and said, "But I'm guessing that it's not because we're getting married that we need to talk to animal people, is it? Unless, of course, you're expanding the wedding party to include alpacas and teacup pigs? Are you doing that? Because if you are I have to say it's going to be able to find them matching attire at such short notice?"

I was now grinning at the image of animals in our wedding party, and the tightness in my chest about this new murder research angle had subsided. "Now that you mention it," I said and let my voice trail off. "But no, as fun that idea sounds, I don't think I'm up for holding my bouquet and a tether during the ceremony. I need to have one hand free for yours."

"Fair enough. So then what's with the animals?"

I explained how I had thought that the people who did business with Penelope might have some light to shed on the situation and asked what he thought.

"That is a good idea," he said and then paused. "But I've just brought in our other two suspects from the reviews, and Tuck is wrapped up in a Board Of Supervisors budget meeting all day." He stopped speaking and let the silence spin out.

"Are you asking me if I can do a little investigative work on the police departments behalf, Deputy _____?"

"Did you hear me say that, Harvey Beckett?" I could hear the smile in his voice.

"No, of course not," I said. "This is serious police work."

"Yes, yes it is, and it must be done with the utmost caution. And any serious investigation requires two witnesses to statements, so if I was to do it, I'd have to wait for Tuck to be free."

"Understood. You and Tuck are not available today. " I laughed quietly. "I will not update you at dinner tonight," I said with a laugh and hung up.

Time to see if Mart had a few hours to go sleuthing with me.

ONE OF THE wonderful things about being a consultant like Mart or a business owner like me was that we had flexibility in the way we spent our time. Sometimes, people mistook that flexibility for constant availability or lack of work ethic, but the truth is that Mart and I both worked more hours than most people who had a typical 8-5 job. And while we had flexible time, we also didn't have sick time or vacation time. These were trade offs we were happy to make, especially on days when we had something we wanted to do – like interview animal people – but they didn't come without a cost.

And yet, there was a certain zip that went through me when I double-checked to be sure Marcus was good to cover for the afternoon and then ducked out. It kind of felt like those days when my mom took me out of school early to go to the dentist but then we still had extra time, before everyone else got out of school, to get ice cream or go to the bookstore or something. Clearly Mart felt the same way because when I texted her, her response was only, "!!! Give me 30 minutes!!!"

I grinned as I slid my phone into my back pocket and finished my walk home. That gave me just enough time to make notes and check in with Mom about wedding stuff, something I both really wanted to do and dreaded, mostly because it would mean I had to hear about a lot of the details that I didn't really care about, like the rehearsal schedule. As far as I was concerned, if the people I loved were there in a place I adored with the man I wanted to spend the rest of my life with, I was good.

Fortunately, Mart's knock on our door meant I had an excuse to end the call with Mom just as she began to fill me in on the rehearsal dinner menu that she and Jared's mom had created. I managed to hear something about a nacho bar before I said, "You have it well under control, Mom. Thank you. But I have to go now. Talk to you later" and hung up before she could protest. It was a bit rude, but it was also more than a bit necessary.

Mart still knocked at our front door when she came over, something I had assured her she could just come on it. "Never know what I might see with you love birds," she said every time, but I knew it was more than potential embarrassment that kept her knocking. She and I had been roommates for a long time in her house, and while she had assured me I'd always have a place with her if I needed one, I knew she was glad that her boyfriend Symeon could move in and expect the same privacy she afforded Jared. It was a gentle, quiet thing, but an important one for both of us, this boundary.

So as soon as I hung up with (on?) Mom, I came out to the front porch with a list of vets, groomers, and one ferrier that I hoped we could see that day, and Mart snatched it out of my hand. "You drive. I'll navigate." Before we even got in the car, she was pecking addresses into her phone to plan our most efficient route.

Our first three stops, at the ferrier's house since he lived further away from town and then at the two vet offices on the way back had proven fruitless. While one of the vet techs had heard of Penelope – or her reputation rather – no one had any particular interaction with her or the spa.

"This is a little frustrating," Mart said between turning directions to our next stop, a grooming shop on the east side of St. Marin's. "Do you think people are holding back because they know about the murder?"

I shrugged. "Could be. But I didn't get any sense anyone was hiding anything. Did you?" When she shook her head, I said, "Plus, have you ever known small-town folk to avoid gossip, even if they have to say, 'I don't usually talk about people like this' before they talk about people like that?"

Mart chuckled. "Well, you have a point there. And when we first moved here, I hated that, felt like everybody was up in my business. But now, I kind of like that people keep tabs on me. It means they care."

"They do, sometimes just about the best story to tell at the diner on Friday, but they do care," I said with a laugh. "Okay, so what do we know about this groomer?"

"She's young, maybe early 20s. Grew up here. Went to beauty school but decided she wanted to work with animals." Mart was staring at her phone. "She has some great photos of dogs with some wild hair-dos here." She turned the phone toward me as we reached a stoplight. "Look at this pink mohawk on this Scottish Terrier."

"Oh, we'll need to tell Cate and Luke that Sasquatch needs a new do." Our friends had the most laid-back, warm-natured Scottie I'd ever met. Somehow, a pink mohawk felt like an awkward fit for him, and I said so to Mart. "Maybe she could wax his moustache instead?"

"That would be perfect," she replied. "This is it." She pointed to a classic Winnebago set back from the road and surrounded by pots and flower beds. "Looks like she's a gardener."

"Good," I said. "We can talk plants to break the ice." Jared and Elle both had taught me a lot about gardening in the past two years, and as I scanned the planters while walking to the door, I saw that Annette, the groomer, had the remnants of a great cottage garden there.

"Good afternoon," a tall, thin black woman with long braids said as she opened the door and extended her hand to Mart. "I'm Annette Gooden." She glanced behind us and paused. "Do you have an appointment." Her eyes darted to the small "Annette's Animals Grooming" sign beside the door.

I stepped forward a bit and said, "Oh, I'm sorry. We don't. I'm Harvey Beckett. I own the bookshop in town. We were hoping we could ask you a couple of questions about Penelope _____. Do you have any space before your next appointment?"

Annette's previously open face had gone completely rigid at the sound of Penelope's name, but she still nodded and let us into a very stylish single-wide complete with a waiting room and a coffee bar. "Please take a seat," she said, pointing to the banquette on the far wall as she sat gracefully in the driver's seat in the cab next to the wash station, which was a waist-high walk-in tub custom-fit to the place where the passenger's seat would have been originally.

"Your workspace is so inventive," I said with genuine enthusiasm. "Wow. A small space with all the necessaries."

My compliment seemed to re-warm Annette a bit, and she said, "Well, it's all I really need, right here?" She gestured around the camper. "Not everyone wants to live and work in the same space, but I like the simplicity of it."

"Oh, you live here, too?" Mart said as she glanced toward the back of the trailer. "I can see how that might be nice." I knew Mart was lying through her teeth. That woman could not survive in such a small space for even a day, but still, I appreciated her effort to keep the congenial conversation.

Annette smiled. "Yeah. You said you wanted to talk with me about Penelope?" Her face got guarded again. "I'm not sure what I can tell you. We were, as she saw it, competitors, and so I didn't have much interaction with her that wasn't based on business."

"You didn't see her as your competition?" I asked, curious about her phrasing.

"Not at all," she said without pause. "She definitely gears her business toward the tourists and such. Maybe some of the folks who live in town, but my clients are old St. Marinites, country people mostly, who want a good price on good service."

"With an occasional pink mohawk thrown in," Mart said with a smile.

"Ah, you've looked at my website. Yes, sometimes, we're able to give our pets more care than we give ourselves," she said quietly. "I try to do new cuts and even nails for people who pour themselves into their pets but can't afford the fancier salons."

There was definitely a tinge of something in Annette's voice. Jealousy? Animosity? Something, but she was also right. I had known a lot of lonely people who took great joy in gussying up their dogs and cats, even one guinea pig, as a mood lifter for both of them. "That's a great service," I said, "and probably something Penelope didn't offer."

Annette laughed out loud. "Are you kidding? Penelope wouldn't have ever deigned to do anything but the most traditional, pretentious grooming job. She was not inclined toward whimsy."

"Say more about that?" Mart asked, picking up, I'm sure, on the touch of what I now saw was scorn in Annette's words.

The groomer took a deep breath, and when she spoke again, her voice was a bit softer. "It's just a difference of purpose, I guess. I want people and their animals to feel good about themselves. Penelope seemed to want to help people make their animals showpieces for their lifestyle."

"Like *Best In Show*?" Mart said suddenly. "Have you seen that?"

Annette grinned. "One of my favorites. And yes, just like that."

"You're more of the Christopher Guest and the bloodhound type then?" I added.

This made Annette's smile broaden even more. "Exactly. I'm much more a Harlan Pepper and Hubert kind of groomer."

I sighed. "I can see what you mean. Penelope leaned more toward the Parker Posey type?"

"Oh my goodness, I'd never thought of that, but yes." Annette grew quiet. "I'm sorry she is dead, just as I'd be sorry for anyone who died. But I can't say it won't make my life a bit easier."

"How so?" Mart said.

Annette sighed. "She was always trying to undercut me. If I offered a special, she'd offer the same, at just a few dollars cheaper. When I started offering herbal treatments for my customers and their pets, she did the same."

"Ah, yes, the garden out front. I saw the remains of echinacea and mint, some sage," I said. "You grew the herbs yourself?"

"I did, mostly because I love to garden, and it's cheaper that way. But she brought in a trained herbalist and started offering special packages that took away some of my customers. Ever since she's opened, I've had a hard time making ends meet." She paused and looked at her hands. "Still, no one deserves to be killed."

I glanced over at Mart who met my gaze. The fact that Penelope had been murdered was all over the news, so it wasn't that surprising that Annette knew. Still, there was something weighty about the fact that she'd brought up the murder specifically.

"I hear you," I said, "and while we never wish anyone misfortune, of course, there is nothing wrong with making use of this time to build our business . . . if that's what you want to do."

"That is what I want to do, but I feel horrible about it. Taking advantage of someone's misfortune that way." Annette's voice was scratchy as she spoke.

"I think," said Mart, "that the idea of 'taking advantage' has been maligned. You are doing nothing wrong to fill a void, to offer people who need a service that service. Unless you killed Penelope, you have nothing to feel terrible about."

I suppressed a wince as Mart flat out mentioned the possibility that Annette had committed murder, but Annette didn't seem to notice. Instead, she smiled gently at Mart.

"Thank you for that." She glanced over at me. "Was that all you wanted to ask? If Penelope and I got along?"

"No, actually. We figured you didn't. She didn't seem to get along with anyone," I said. "We were wondering if you knew anything about anyone who really had a bone to pick with her? Anyone who was really angry or such?"

"You want me to tell you if I know who might have killed her?" Annette said, her eyes wide.

I could have hemmed and hawed, tried to downplay my intention, but already I knew that Annette was too savvy for that. "Yes, we do."

She sighed and said, "Check with Steve Sutton. Last time I saw him, he was going on and on about how Penelope had injured one of his patients during one of her treatments. He was pretty livid."

"Steve Sutton the vet?" Mart asked. "Do you think he'd do something to Penelope?"

Annette shrugged. "He's definitely got a temper, especially when it comes to how people treat animals."

"Don't we all," I said quietly.

"Of course," Annette said, "but do you slash the tires of people who don't care for their pets like you think they should?"

I had to admit my disgust for animal neglect and abuse wasn't strong enough to drive me to vandalism. "No, I do not."

With a tilt of her head, Annette stood. "It was nice to meet you both, but I have a cocker spaniel who needs a good ear cleaning on her way. If you need anything else, you know where to find me."

Mart and I stood and followed her to the door. As I stepped

onto her small stoop, I said, "I like how you've left the stalks and seeds standing for winter."

"Got to feed the birds, you know?" Annette said before waving and closing the door.

"That was interesting," Mart said as we got into the car.

"Sure was," I said. "Sure was."

5

"Where to next?" Mart asked as we pulled back out onto the main road toward town. "Who else do we need to interrogate?" she added in a horrible New York accent.

"Well," I said as I glanced at the dashboard clock, "we probably only have time for one more stop before business hours are over for most everyone, so let's prioritize." I handed her the list that I'd crammed into my pocket.

"Harvey, have you heard of folders? Or a purse? Anything that holds things neatly?" she said as she smoothed out the rumpled paper.

"Hey be grateful I don't write all my notes on my hands and arms anymore. That practice carried me through my 20s just fine."

Mart rolled her eyes hard enough that I could see it in my peripheral vision but then said, "Okay, so there are the two vets in town on here. One of them is ours, and I can't see her even caring what Penelope WhatsherFace did."

I nodded. Our vet was old Eastern Shore stock. Totally up to date on the latest information and technologies but also quite confident that the old ways worked well in most cases. I loved her because I knew she'd tell me the brazen truth with compassion, and she also wasn't one to recommend expensive procedures if there weren't going to meaningful improve an animal's life. "Yeah, Melissa is brass tacks and no nonsense. I think we can skip her."

Mart took a pen out of her very cute and tidy purse and marked through our vet's name. "So that just leaves that mobile cat grooming van and the vet right in town. Maybe we do the vet since that's most on the way?"

I nodded. "Sounds good. I'll try to catch up with the other groomer tomorrow. Maybe someone will let me borrow a cat as cover?"

"Good luck with that," Mart said.

Within a few minutes, we had pulled into a very well-land-scaped, very lovely farmhouse that had been, apparently, converted into a vet's office. The pathway up to the front porch was lined with plants and adorable animal figurines made from concrete, and on the porch itself, hand-painted Styrofoam coolers were tucked along the sides.

"Interesting décor?" Mart said as she peered down at one of the coolers and then promptly stumbled backward. "There's a cat in there!"

I leaned forward. "Oh, hi kitty," I said and was greeted with a fervent hiss. "Alright, then, enjoy your bed."

We turned toward the and saw a brass sign that said, "Come on in." We did as we were directed and stepped into a beautiful foyer with a beautiful staircase at the back and a receptionist's desk straight ahead.

"Hello," I said to the smiling woman at the desk. "We were wonderful if Dr. Stoltzfus has a few minutes to chat with us."

"He's with a patient at the moment, but when he's free, I'm happy to ask him. May I tell him what this is about?"

I opened my mouth to say Penelope's name, but Mart spoke before I could. "We've found a few stray cats, and we're hoping to get his advice on how to care for them best."

The woman's face grew even brighter. "Oh, I'm sure he'll be happy to talk with you. If you'll take a seat, I'll let you know when he's free." She gestured toward a sitting room that looked more like a Victorian parlor than a waiting room. "There's kombucha and water if you're thirsty."

We made our way into the room and I did, having never tried it, pour myself some of the kombucha stored in the small fridge in the corner. It seemed a strange element for this tidy, farm-like office, but we all had our eccentricities. And the drink was good, if slightly sweaty tasting. "Want some?" I said as I held my glass out to Mart.

"No thank you. I know it's really good for you, but I can't stand it. Tastes like the locker room in my middle school gym."

I had to admit her description was pretty accurate, and I wondered what it said about me that I kind of liked it. I carried my glass to a lovely armchair across from the one Mart had chosen and glanced at the magazines on the table between us. *Dogs Naturally, Holistic Wellness,* and several other alternative medicine titles. The kombucha was beginning to fit more.

And when the vet joined us, it felt like everything clicked into place. He was a white man in his 50s with a long black ponytail and socks under his sandals. I totally got the vibe when I saw him. "Dr. Stoltzfus?" I said as I stood up. "Thanks for agreeing to meet with us."

"Of course," he said as he shook both our hands. "I understand you know of some stray cats?"

"Um, yes," Mart said as I shot her a look. She'd started this, so she was going to have to carry it through. "I mean, yes, by my friend's bookstore downtown there are several strays. We've been sure to give them water, but we haven't fed them because we aren't sure it's the best call for them to be where there's so much traffic."

I stared at my best friend. She was a very good li--, story-teller. A very good storyteller.

"Do you think we should call animal control, just to be sure they're safe? Or is there another option?"

The doctor nodded seriously and then said, "It sounds like you have a feral cat colony, much like I do here." He pointed toward the porch. "You probably saw the coolers when you came in."

"We did," I said. "So the cats in those are feral?"

"Yes, and they live right around here. We give them food and water and those boxes to stay warm or cool, depending. And they keep mice and rats away." He studied first me and then Mart. "I would be happy to help you give your own colony safety if you'd like."

Now, I was feeling bad. This man was offering to help us, and we didn't even have any stray cats. "But is it really safe to encourage them to stay in such a high-traffic area?"

Stoltzfus sighed. "Probably not, but the truth is that if you move them anywhere else, they'll likely just return. That's home to them." He held my gaze for a very long moment. "And the only other option is just not an option at all, as far as I'm concerned."

My heart started to pound. "Euthanasia?" I asked.

"Cat murder," he said.

Mart jerked her head back at that pronouncement but recovered my nodding sincerely. "So what do you suggest?"

For the next few minutes, we listened to him explain how spaying and neutering were essential as were safe havens for the cats. He offered a very discounted rate for the sterilization procedures and said he'd give us a list of people who often supported feral cat colonies. "It's a bit of work upfront, but then, the colony provides a service. And when the males are neutered, it's a fairly peaceable kingdom, if you will."

I figured now wasn't the time to mention that I brought two dogs to work who would, if allowed, do anything they could to disturb that peace. Besides, we didn't have any cats to speak of. "That sounds great, Dr. Stoltzfus," I said. "Much better than the earlier advice we'd been given."

"Oh?" he asked. "What advice was that?"

Mart shook her head. "That woman who owns the cat spa, well, she told us to just have them put down. That they were simply a nuisance."

At the mere mention of Penelope, Stoltzfus's face grew hard and his whole body tensed. "That woman," he practically spat as he spoke, "should never have been allowed to touch an animal. How anyone could trust her with their beloved pets I'll never know."

I nodded. "That's the impression we got when we told her about the cats." Since we were all in on this lie, I figured why not just goad him a bit, see what he said. "I thought that when she added reiki to her spa that she might have been, well . . . " I paused and looked at my now empty glass of kombucha, "like-minded, you know?"

"She added reiki? Really? That is rather enlightened." Dr. Stoltzfus seemed to be considering his earlier opinion, but after a moment, he sighed. "I imagine it was just a business ploy on her part, not a real knowledge of the practice." His words were clipped and dismissive. Clearly there wasn't much room in his opinion of Penelope to even allow for things he valued.

"Apparently," Mart said and stood up. "Thank you for your time. We'll begin our plans for the, um, colony did you call it?"

"Yes," the vet said brightening. "Here's my card. Just call anytime if you need advice or to schedule procedures."

I took his card and then followed Mart back out the door to our car.

"Well, if ever someone was a suspect, Dr. Walter "Kombucha" Stoltzfus is the man," Mart said as I started the car.

I snorted with laughter. I had to give it to my friend. She had a way with words.

WHEN WE GOT BACK to my place, Jared was grilling something that smelled amazing out on the back patio.

"Dear God, you're marrying a good man," Mart said as she caught the scent on our way up the porch steps. "I love pizza, but something about grilling just pings a visceral pleasure in me."

"Wow, you're eloquent about food today," I said.

"Today? Do you know what I do for a living? If I can't describe the new wine with at least 18 adjectives, I'm not doing my job right." She glanced over at me as I held the front door open for me. "Don't tell Symeon what I said about pizza, okay?"

I nodded just as I caught sight of Symeon coming around the corner with two glasses of wine. "Did I hear my name?"

Mart stretched up and kissed him. "What smells so good?" she said when she landed back on her heels. Always adroit at changing the subject, that one.

"Jared is trying out some steak marinade that he read in one of his cooking magazines. Invited us over for dinner. Want to stay?" Symeon said.

"Are you kidding?" Mart replied. "You'd have to drag me out of here now."

"Good," I said. "Just the four of us?" I asked Symeon.

"Tuck and Lu are coming, too," he said. "I heard mention of a hypothetical not-investigation you two were pursuing today." He winked at me. "Can't wait to hear about it."

"Let me tell you," I said. "We have a story to tell."

By the time Jared had finished grilling, the twice-baked

potatoes were just coming out of the oven, thanks to Symeon, and we had a gorgeous pot of lima beans with ham hock to go with them. "Looks amazing," Lu said as she carried in her own contribution, a pineapple upside down cake that seemed to be dripping with syrup.

"I am famished," Tuck said as he took off his ball cap and hung it on the back of one of our dining room chairs. "What can I do to help?"

"I think we're almost set," Jared said. "But you can get folks drink orders."

Tuck opened the refrigerator door and then took a look at the wine rack on the counter. "Sweet tea. Water. Chardonnay. Or Pinot noir," he said.

"Nix the chardonnay," Mart added. "Not robust enough with the steak."

"I'll take sweet tea," I said. "Can't have a migraine this week." The sulfites in red wine often gave me days-long headaches that left me barely able to function, so I'd sworn off the reds for the most part. But I also trusted Mart's judgement about wine. If she said Chardonnay wasn't a good pairing, it wasn't a good pairing

"Pinot for me," Mart said. "I'll drink your glass," she added as she winked at me.

The other four gave their orders and before long, the six of us were seated with a delicious, family-style meal set on the table before us. For a few minutes, we chatted about our lives, the goings on in town, and such. Apparently, as Tuck informed us, there was a major kerfuffle happening at the high school because the athletic director had brought in an artist to update the mural on the outside of the gym. Someone from the 1950s had painted it, and it, as I could personally attest, looked like it had been created by members of the KKK. All the athletes in it were white and blonde, and the proportions of some of them were much like a kindergartner would draw. It was time for a refresh.

"Let me guess. That mural was commissioned by someone's granddaddy, and it's now considered sacred in St. Marin's lore," Mart suggested.

"You nailed it," Tuck said. "But the AD gets to make decisions about the athletics facilities, so it's really a pointless fight. I expect, however, we'll see protesters when they begin work next week."

"Lord almighty," I said. "Have they nothing better to do with their time?"

Every pair of eyes at the table turned and stared at me.

"Right. Right. This is St. Marin's, so no, they have nothing better to do unless there's a fire to chase when they hear about it on their scanners," I said.

"Now, there's an idea," Jared noted with a glance at Tuck, who smiled widely.

"Best not reveal your trade secrets," Lu remarked, "you're already delegating some of your duties to outside forces." She smiled at Mart and me. "Find out anything interesting."

"Well, first of all, if anyone asks, we have a feral cat colony downtown," Mart said.

Tuck nodded. "We *do* have a feral cat colony downtown. The sheriff's office has been caring for it for years." He raised an eyebrow. "But why is that relevant?"

"Well," I said, "your girl Martha here." I winked at Mart who *hated* her full name. "Your girl is a masterful liar, and she has convinced a local vet that we have a feral cat colony that we needed advice on."

All eyes turned to Mart, and she, rather proudly, I must say, related the full tale of our afternoon adventures, beginning with her rather masterful story at Dr. Stoltzfus's office and wrapping up with a much less exciting and therefore much shorter recount of our time at Annette Gooden's.

Tuck and Jared exchanged a look. "So basically, they both had problems with Penelope?"

I nodded. "Seems like it, although I will say that Stoltzfus was much, much angrier, at least visibly, than Gooden." I shook my head. "I know that doesn't necessary correlate to the likelihood of who committed the murder, but I will say that it was a much intenser experience--

"In all the ways," Mart added.

"Yes, in all ways with Stoltfus than with Gooden." I knew both of these officers valued my intuition, but I also knew that they would need hard evidence to proceed with anything we'd told them.

"Well," Tuck said, "I think it's about time for you to put on one of your infamous benefits, Harvey."

I sighed almost as heavily as Jared did. "Really? Right now. You do know we're getting married this weekend?" he said.

"I do, and I don't think this has to be a big deal, maybe just something casual, a sort of memorial to honor Penelope by doing a bit of fundraising for feral cats?" Tuck batted his eyelashes at me just long enough that his wife smacked his arm.

"Tucker Mason. I thought you only used that trick on me," she said. Then, turning to me, "If you're good with it, Harvey, I'll just use your store but take care of the entire event myself. Maybe we could even do it tomorrow? I can put out a quick press release, and Tuck here can help me with the details since he's the feral cat expert at the table."

"Good," Mart said. "You need Styrofoam coolers."

Everyone but me stared at her for a long moment until she said, "They make good insulated habitats for the cats. What?! They do."

"She's right. That's what Stoltzfus recommended. He even said he had some folks who liked to donate them for just this purpose."

Lu took out her phone. "Alright then, I'll call him first thing tomorrow. We'll plan to do the food and, um, cooler drive from 3-5 tomorrow. It's supposed to be a nice day, and I"ll have churros from the truck for anyone who donates."

"If I brought my portable oven and sold pizzas with 100% of the profits going to the cause would that help?" Symeon asked.

"That would be amazing," Lu said as she continued to type into her phone. "Maybe we could close off Main St. for those two hours." This time she batted her eyes at her husband.

He rolled his but said, "Fine. We'll make it an impromptu town party."

"All this sounds amazing," I added, "but what do you need me to do?"

Everyone at the table said, in total unison, "Nothing." They were so adamant that I bounced back against my chair.

"Alright, then. Thanks." I didn't really feel grateful – I hated to miss out – but I knew they were looking after me.

"In fact," Jared said, "You and I are taking the next two days off. Marcus has the store covered, and Tuck has assured me that all is good with the station. We have a wedding to finish getting ready for."

"What?!" I said. "Really?" I suddenly felt near tears, and I realized it was because I had been trying to do all the things. But for once, I didn't really want to do everything. I just wanted to prepare this amazing man so we could have an amazing day. "Okay," I said through a tight throat. "That sounds really good."

"Great," Mart said. "Your mom and I will be focus on wedding plans and keep you updated. You two do what you need to do for the big day, and Lu and Tuck, maybe you can recruit the rest of the crew to help with the event tomorrow?"

"Already on it," Lu said as she held up her phone at the same moment all of ours chimed. "The crew is recruited."

That night, for the first one in a few weeks, I actually fell asleep without having to pull out a pen and paper to write down all the to-dos swimming in my head. Jared and I leisurely cleaned up from dinner and then sat out on the front porch to talk about our plans for the next two days. Then, I drifted off peacefully with the confidence that 48-hours was more than enough time to finish wedding prep, hold a fundraiser, and solve a murder. We had this.

6

A pparently, my subsconscious did not feel as confident as my outer self did because I dreamed all night of wild cats and tulle (which was weird because we didn't have any tulle in the wedding) and grasping hands. But still, despite the nightmares, I work up feeling pretty rested and ready for the day.

Jared had insisted I turn off notifications on my phone last night, so when I had my coffee in hand and finally opened my texts, I saw that the crew was well into planning for the afternoon. "Harvey," Mart's latest message said. "You can come, but only if you promise to just hang out. You cannot work."

"Got it," I replied and decided my best bet was to mute that text thread so that I could actually abide by that request. I kind of wanted to turn off my phone altogether, but I knew that would make my mother lose her mind.

Jared woke just long enough after me that I was able to get a couple of chapters read in my new novel, *The Astonishing Color Of After*. It was a book I'd been wanting to read for a long time, mostly because it was on all the lists of recommended magical realism books, but only now was I making time for it. And it was splendid.

So splendid in fact that when Jared came out of the bedroom all sparkling and good-smelling from his shower, I had to make a concerted effort to put the book down, even though this was my favorite time of day to hug him. He just was so fresh first thing in the morning.

After a few more sentences, the urge to hug him overcame my interest in the book, and I gave him a giant squeeze and said, "What are we making for breakfast, Almost Husband?"

He smiled and squeezed me closer as he said, "How does baked oatmeal sound?"

"Delicious, but do we have time for that," I asked. "We do when I made it yesterday and just have to heat it up."

"What? How did you--? Never mind. I don't know how you continue to surprise me with such perfect things, but I"ll take it . . . for the rest of my life if you don't mind."

"I don't mind at all." He led me back to my reading chair and said, "One more chapter while I get it ready."

My heart tightened in just the best way. "Thank you," I whispered and watched him walk back to the kitchen, that fiancé of mine.

OUR BELLIES full of delicious baked oatmeal and berries and me finally showered and dressed for the day, we went over our to-do list for the wedding. We decided to save the last of the yard work, which was really minimal given Elle's intervention, until this evening after the fundraiser since it would make us kind of sweaty and dirty, most likely. And instead, focused on the gifts we were making for our wedding party.

We both wanted these to be really special because the people standing up with us were, well, really special, so we'd decided to handcraft a journal for each of them. Jared had gathered a stack of vintage books from thrift stores, and I had pulled together the glue, paper, and ribbons, and together we'd learned how to turn old books that no one wanted to read into beautiful, bespoke journals that were designed for each of our friends.

The journals were complete, but now we had to inscribe them to each person, a task which I had been thinking about for weeks now. Fortunately, I had made notes on each person, and so when Jared and I sat down at the dining room table with our stacks of journals, I was able to start straight in on my personalized message for each of our friends. I cried the whole time, and I'm pretty sure I saw Jared wipe a tear away as well. But within the hour, we were both done.

Good thing, too, because a knock sounded on our door mid-morning, and there were my mother, father, and Mart, arms laden with flowers and ribbon of their own. "Good morning," I said.

"Is it?" Mom said. "It has to be at least 2pm doesn't it?" She looked very tired but also very happy.

"How long have you been up, Mom?" I said as Jared and I took the things from everyone's arm and slid them onto the now empty table. Jared must have quickly hidden the journals – a good man since they were to be a surprise at the rehearsal dinner tomorrow.

"Oh just 3. I wanted to get a good start before the world did." She smiled. "Any chance you have any coffee?"

"I was just about to make a new pot," Jared said. "Hugh want to help."

Once, I had told Jared about how I hated that most men always assumed the women around them would do the things in the kitchen and shared how my dad, as good as man as he was, often did that. Now, every time there was cooking or cleaning to be done and Dad was around, Jared recruited him to assist. Dad always agreed without protest because, well, how

could he not. I felt like we'd struck a blow against the patri-
archy in this small way.

"Okay," I said to Mart and Mom. "What is all this? And do
we need to get these flowers into water?"

"Yes, do you have any buckets?" Mom asked.

"Maybe, but what if we used vases instead?" I asked.
"They're actually right here." I turned to one of the built-in
cabinets in the dining room and began to pass vases to Mart.
"We have a few."

"I'll say," Mart said as she slid the ninth one onto the table.
"Why so many?"

"You did well, Harvey," Mom said. "I asked her to begin
gathering them when she saw them at yard sales and such.
These are going to be our centerpieces for the wedding."

I smiled. When Mom had first told me her idea about the
eclectic décor for the wedding, I had been a bit worried that it
would seem too casual. But once I'd seen her intention to do
the flowers in matching arrangements with matching bows, I
understood that what she was imagining was just what I
wanted – a low environmental impact and a high visual one.

"We have more, too, if we need them. I just couldn't fit them
all in here," I said with a wave of my arm toward the cabinet.
"And the candle holders are in that cabinet, Mom, when you're
ready for them."

"Perfect," Mom said. "Let's get the flowers into water, and
while I arrange those, you girls can put the candles in."

I smiled. No way was my mother going to let me do
anything visual if she had her choice. She and I had both
learned, long ago, that I was good with words and numbers, not
so much with anything visually aesthetic. "Sounds good, Mom."

Mart and I trotted into the kitchen with our arms full of
vases, and after we filled them, we all made trips back to the
dining room table to get them to Mom along with her cup of
coffee. For the next hour, the five of us managed to follow

Mom's orders to the letter by cutting ribbons, placing candles, and eventually tucking all the arrangements into our downstairs bathroom where we could keep them cool and dark until tomorrow night.

That task completed, Mart said she needed to be off to get a bit of work done before she headed to the fundraiser at 3. "I'll be keeping an eye on you, Harvey Beckett. No work."

I raised my hand and said, "I solemnly swear that I will just eat pizza and churros and pet cats."

"Good," Mart said and saluted as she went out the door.

"Now what?" Jared said as he finished what I noticed was his fourth cup of coffee. He was feeling the stress, too.

"Now, Hugh and I head into town to do the things we need to do, and the two of you have to take this and go to Easton." She handed Jared a golden envelope.

"Are we going to see Willy Wonka?" he asked with a grin.

"Better," Dad said. "We'll see you at 3 at the store."

I stared at my parents quizzically, but they just smiled and left without another word.

"Well, what is it?" I said as soon as the door closed.

Jared slipped a finger under the seal of the envelope and tore it open. Then, he pulled out a long piece of cardstock and read, "90 minute couples massage for the almost newlyweds. Relax."

"Isn't a couples massage something people usually do on the honeymoon?" I asked.

"Maybe, but we're not really having a honeymoon yet, and to be honest, this makes a bit more sense. We're super stressed and busy *before* the wedding, so why not go now?" He smiled at me. "You ready?"

I stared at him blankly for a minute. "Um, yeah, I guess. I just need to check in with Marc--."

"Nope, you don't. Marcus has got everything at the store

covered and you will see him in just a few hours anyway. Let that go." He leaned over and kiss my cheek.

"Great, now I'll be singing Elsa's song all afternoon." I wondered if all of North America had been ruined for that phrase because of that movie. "But you're right. He's got it. Let's do this."

Jared smiled and held the door open. "You know, you just missed a perfect opportunity to curse me with the song, too."

"I know," I said as I put my arm through his. "I'm just nicer than you are."

7

The commitment I made to myself after our massage was to do that once a month for the rest of my life. I didn't really get anything special out of having a stranger massage me while another stranger massaged Jared – that part actually felt weird – but the massage itself was amazing. When we finished, I could barely bend to put my shoes on, my legs were so relaxed, but I felt mentally clearer than I had in a few days.

"That was amazing," Jared said as we headed back out to his car. "We owe your parents' a big thanks."

"We do," I said, "but having two hours of free rein with the wedding plans might have been thanks enough for my mom."

"You aren't wrong."

WE MADE it back to St. Marin's just in time to see Tuck putting the cones up at the end of Main Street for the block party. "Need help, Sheriff?" Jared asked as he pulled up alongside his boss.

"No, sir. You are on vacation until Monday. You just enjoy

the party." He smiled and tipped his cap as we drove to the alley and parked behind my store.

When I let us in the back door, I was delighted to see Taco and Mayhem bounding back to us. "How did you guys get here?" I asked.

The two dopes looked up at me like I was made of bacon, and I sat down right there on the floor to scratch their ears, their favorite bit of attention, especially for Taco who moaned the whole time.

The supposed sound of a basset in distress apparently carried because a few moments later, Marcus appeared. "Oh good, it's you." He smiled at me. "I thought maybe Taco had gotten his ear caught in the backroom door again."

I winced. The poor guy had had these droopy ears all his life, and still he managed to not only get any kind of food he ate on them but also caught them, infrequently in things, like doors. The sound he made then, though, could raise the dead. "Nope, just giving some loving," I replied. "All good here?"

"Yep, just fine. Now, that's the only bit of work you're doing until Monday. The crew is up front if you want to say hi."

Jared, who had leaned against the wall only to find Mayhem leaning against him, said, "Clearly they have rehearsed their lines."

"Clearly." I pulled myself upright again, and having done their greeting duty and appropriate homaged, the two dogs trotted back to their beds in the front window and we followed them to the staging area in Rocky's café.

Everyone we loved was there with streamers billowing behind them or balloons bouncing above them. Obviously, Lu had gone for broke, perhaps literally, on the décor budget. "Nice streamers," I said to Stephen as he breezed past me.

"I'm thinking of entering in rhythmic gymnastics at the next Olympics," he said, doing a very ungraceful pirouette and bumping into Elle in the process, almost spilling her tray full of fresh tulips in bud vases.

"Probably keep your day job," I said to him as I watched Elle place the bright pink and yellow tulips on each table. "They look gorgeous," I whispered as I went to find Rocky and get my afternoon latte. I may not have been working but that didn't mean all my work rituals had to die.

She must have seen me coming – I had to remember to check for cameras – because when I walked over, she set her largest to-go cup on the table in front of me. "Extra shot today. Got to keep you fueled."

I smiled. "But I bet it's decaf."

"Of course, *fueled* and *well-rested* are both crucial." She glanced out the window. "Looks like the cats have arrived."

I turned around and watched as Tucker Mason, our long-time sheriff and dear friend, led a string of cats behind him as he dropped pieces of tuna every few feet. The image was so perfect that I laughed as I dug my phone out of my pocket. "He's like the feline Pied Piper," I said as I moved closer to the window and filmed the scene.

There must have been 30 or 40 cats wandering onto the street from all directions and joining the parade up the double-yellow lines. Tuck, for his part, played the ham he was and waved to the crowd, most of whom had cameras out like I did. He had the royal wave down, I noticed.

For a moment, as I loaded the video to our Instagram page and captioned it, "Sheriff Takes on Fairy Tale Job," I wondered how they were going to keep the cats on the street since it seemed important to someone, Lu, my mom, Mart?, that they be there. But then, I noticed that in front of every door, including my own, people had put out trays of cat food and bowls of water. I'd seen that kind of thing around town here and in other animal-friendly communities, but usually, those things were for dogs. It felt just that the cats were getting their due.

"Pretty awesome, huh?" Mart said as she joined me by the window. "All Lu's idea."

"I like it," I said. "Seeing the cats themselves should make people more generous."

"Agreed. Your dad suggested we get pet store mice and release them so the cats could really prove their worth, but your mother quickly and wisely nixed that idea."

"Mom did always have more common sense than he did." I looked over at the table that Pickle and Bear were setting up on the front walkway. "Anything I can do?"

"Absolutely nothing," Mart said. "I know that will drive you a little crazy, but why don't you just relax by the table and talk to folks? Think of yourself as the official greeter."

I smiled because my friend knew we well. There was no way I was going to be able to just sit around while all this happened, but if I could think of myself as greeting folks, then I had a role, a simple, non-stressful role but a role nonetheless.

"Okay," I said with a smile and made my way to the front door, where Jared was still filming the antics. "Getting some good footage for the department Facebook page?"

"Oh yeah," he replied. "Or for blackmail."

I playfully smacked him on the arm. "And you an officer of the law."

He grinned at me, and I pushed open the front door and took in the sight and sounds. A bevy of cats was streaming to and fro, hissing at anyone who got close but enjoying the various delicacies put out for them. The scent of tuna wafted through the air, and I decided instantly that I preferred the small of salt water by scores. Fortunately, I was able to secure a seat between Lu's food truck and Symeon's pizza oven, and so most of the fishy smell was overcome by the scent of cooking food.

Soon enough, the street was full of people, eating, photographing, and donating to the cause. Stephen and Walter were, as usual, staffing the donation table, and Pickle and Bear had set up what looked to be an hotel laundry trolley to gather anything physical people donated. I could see several Styrofoam coolers already along with a few cases and bags of cat food. This feral cat colony was going to be the most lush one in all of Maryland at this rate.

For a brief moment, I felt a little guilty that our sleuthing had required such an elaborate performance to cover our tracks, but then, I looked at the faces of the people gathered, almost spontaneously, to support a truly worthwhile cause and my guilt evaporated. Maybe St. Marin's had needed this anyway.

Jared pulled up a folding chair next to mine and said, "Good turn out." Then he tilted his head toward the right. "Lots of folks are interested."

I looked where he had gestured and saw Dr. Stoltzfus shaking hands like he was the mayor as he moved through the crowd. I tried to lean back so he wouldn't see me, but he caught my end and headed straight for me. "Heads up," I said quietly to Jared.

He saw the vet just as he walked up to us. "Wow, you move fast," he said as I stood and shook his hand. "I'm glad my ideas inspired you."

My interior voice was formulating some response about him giving himself a lot of credit, but fortunately, my mouth said, "Thank you for the inspiration." I glanced over at Jared and when he gave me a small nod, I said, "This is my fiancé Jared _____. He's a deputy with the sheriff's office, and they've adopted our feral cat colony." I was careful about my choice of tense there. At the very least, I could keep from lying about the cats themselves.

Dr. Stoltzfus shook Jared's hand. "Good man. Keep that wifey happy."

I started to say something, but Jared spoke before I could. "This woman who will soon be my wife makes me very happy, as I do her if she's to be believed. It's a mutal thing no matter what those "happy life" t-shirts say."

A tiny flush spread up the vet's throat. "Of course, of course," he said.

Jared smiled just a little and said, "But you know, it's the women from the new dog spa who really turned out. They rallied the storeowner's support and paid for all the décor."

A muscle ticked in Stoltzfus's jaw. "The dog spa? Penelope Herold's dog spa?"

"Yes, sir," Jared said in his most fake casual tone. His real casual tone didn't have any edge to it like this. "They did it in Penelope's honor, actually. Absolute tragedy what happened to her."

"If you say so," the vet said quickly and then must have realized what he said because he looked over at Jared and continued. "Of course, it's a good thing. These cats deserve the best. Are they who I should talk to about reduced fees spay and neuter services?"

I smiled. "Indeed they are. You can find them at the spa, I think." I hoped I was right.

"I'll go say hello, then," the vet said and headed that direction.

"I didn't know smug could translate into a gait, but there it is," Jared said when he was out of earshot.

I laughed. "So smug. But was what you said true? Did Caro and Sheila really do all that?"

"From what Marcus said, yep. They were apparently very enthusiastic when Lu contacted them." He had a small wrinkle between his brows.

"What's this about?" I said as I gently pressed my finger between his eyebrows.

"I don't know," he said. "Maybe I'm too suspicious, but even if they didn't like their boss, that kind of traumatic experience can really take it out of you. But—"

"You know as well as I do that grief takes all forms," I said. "But I hear you. They're still on the suspect list then?"

Jared nodded. "But enough of that. Let's get churros."

IF ANYTHING, the crowd grew larger as the afternoon went on, and the line for churros was quite long. I had to resist, with a lot of effort, my desire to jump into Lu's truck to help her out, but fortunately, my will power didn't have to last long because her husband joined her to help thin the line. I looked over to see Mart staffing the till for Symeon's pizza line, too. My friends were good people.

Fortunately, Jared and I had managed to snag both churros and pizza before the lines got too long, so well-fed and antsy – neither of us was good at staying out of things; that's part of what made us a good couple – we decided to stroll and see all the sights. And there were many. It seemed, even with only hours' notice, a lot of the shop owners had figured out ways to support the effort – from percentages of proceeds to free items if people showed they'd brought in a donation for the cats.

"Lu is a force," I said as we peeked in Elle's farm store and saw her handed out free tulips to people who showed their donation receipt. "She really rallied the troops."

"Yes, yes she did." He pulled me into a quick hug. "Look alive. Annette Gooden is walking this way." He pecked my cheek and stepped back with a smile as he gently spun me back in the direction we had been heading.

I was glad for the heads up, even if it only bought me a

second or two, because Gooden looked angry, and she was looking right at me.

"What is this?" she said. "You didn't say anything about an animal benefit when you came by earlier. Were you trying to close me out of the chance to help?"

"What?! No," I said. "I didn't even know about this event until after we saw you."

"You expect me to believe that," she said. "When it's all your posse working it?"

I put my hands up on the air. "I don't know what to tell you. It apparently came together very fast." I took a deep breath because I was quite livid myself at her accusation and knew that escalating things here was not going to help anything, least of all the investigation. "Annette Gooden, this is my fiancé Deputy Jared _____. We are getting married on Saturday, so we've actually been working on wedding prep all day." No need to tell her that some of that prep included a luxurious massage.

"Oh," she said quietly, the chagrin showing in her expression. "I'm sorry. I think I'm more upset than I realized about Penelope's death."

I studied her for a minute. "But didn't you say you guys didn't get along?"

"We didn't, but she was still a colleague, a neighbor, you know?" She glanced behind her and gestured toward the spa. "And there they are, putting on a show to get business just days after their owners' death."

I looked over at where Sheila and Caro were, indeed, putting on a show by making balloon animals and painting children's faces. They certainly didn't look sad, but then, as I'd just reminded Jared, grief took many forms.

"Maybe this is their way of honoring her?" Jared said, but even he didn't sound convinced.

"Maybe," Gooden replied. "Anyway, I'm sorry. This is a good

cause, and I hope I can help out. Do you know who I can talk to about that?"

I also told her the same thing Jared had told Stoltzfus but decided that sending her to chat with Caro and Sheila wasn't our best bet. Instead, I pointed back toward where Mart stood by the pizza oven. "See that woman there with the long brown hair. That's Mart. She's helping coordinate things. You could let her know how you'd like to chip in."

"Great," she said. "I figured some of these guys might be in rough shape and could use a good shampoo and nail trim. Happy to donate my services." She smiled. "Sorry, again. It's just a lot, all of this." She gestured to the street. "Have a good day."

8

A s she walked toward the dog spa, Jared and I made our way back to my store, choosing silently not to discuss what had just happened. It was, as Annette had said, all a little too much to make sense of at the moment.

Inside All Booked Up, things were steady, and Marcus was talking with a young girl about his deep affection for the Captain Underpants books. She seemed delighted by the idea of a villain named Professor Poopy Pants, and I was pleased to see that her mother, although apparently slightly disgusted, didn't object when she said she wanted to ge the first two in the series. I expected they'd both end up loving them.

Our newest college student hire was working the register, and things seemed to be well under control. And since I wasn't allowed to work today, I had a brainstorm. "Do you want to sit in here and look at books and magazines with me like we're customers?" I asked Jared.

He looked over and smiled. "I love that idea. I'll get us two decaf lattes, and you find the spot?"

"Deal," I said and headed right to the place I imagined myself reading when I had a chance to daydream a bit. The two wingback chairs next to the fiction section were some of my favorites, and when I rounded the corner and saw them, I was thrilled to find them empty. I quickly laid my scarf on one of them in the universal symbol for "reserved" and went to grab a few magazines I knew Jared and I would like. This felt like such a treat.

One of the ways I had survived some pretty dark days in my life was by going to a local bookstore, grabbing a stack of magazines and books, and sipping a latte while I perused them. I hadn't always had the money to buy, and while I could have browsed – and often did – at the library, there was just something about being out amongst people and their store energy that lifted my spirits a bit. Throw in a latte, and I was in heaven.

So when I'd opened my own store, I'd committed to allowing my customers that same privilege, encouraging it even with the comfy chairs and little signs that mentioned that browsing was awesome. Sometimes, sure, a book got damaged with a coffee ring or a torn page, but I didn't mind that. Books are objects that are both frail and rugged, and they are meant to be used. So what if they got used before they were paid for. I was confident that the atmosphere of the store encouraged people to buy a great deal more than they would if they had to simple treat the books like museum objects until they'd paid. Those sales more than made up for damages.

And here I was, a copy of *Southern Cottage* in my lap and my feet on a stool. I could hear the shoppers talking about book, and the scent of coffee from Rocky's café filled the air. It was lovely, and for the first time, I was just in the midst of it as another reader instead of the owner. Delightful.

When Jared joined me, he picked up *Fine Woodworking* and began to read. My fiancé was not much of a browser about anything, I'd learned. If he was going to give his time to something, he was going to do it with intention. I wasn't that way myself, but I admired the trait in him. As I watched him read for a few seconds, I wondered what delightful projects might adorn our own home soon and felt the tingle of excitement about our life together zip through me again.

A few minutes later, when I was deep into studying the photos of a delightful cottage garden with stepping stones surrounded by moss, someone said my name. I looked up to see Toggle there, her arms full of art books.

"Sorry to bother you," she said brightly. "I just wanted to say Hi."

I smiled at the artist, even as a pit of concern formed in my stomach. "Hi, Toggle. How are you?"

She sighed. "I'm okay. You know, hard week here in town." She looked out the front window. "But this impromptu fair is fun. I even picked up a cooler so I can put it on my fire escape in case the cats need it."

"Oh you live downtown?" I asked and felt Jared shift just slightly in his chair. He knew what I was doing, and he didn't love it.

"Oh yeah, just a couple doors down. Max rents me the apartment of Le Cuisine." She smiled. "The smells that come up the stairway are so good."

I smiled. She wasn't wrong. Max, the restaurant's owner, and I had an interesting history, to say the least, but despite his sometimes gruff demeanor, he had a good heart. Today, I'd noticed that he'd actually cooked up fresh fish and chicken to put in the bowls outside his place. No canned food there.

"How cool," I said even as I wondered why I hadn't known she lived there before today. "Well, we're neighbors then," I said.

She smiled. "We are." Her face grew more serious as she turned to Jared. "Deputy, do you have any more leads on who killed Penelope?"

Jared looked up as if he was slightly startled to be pulled into the conversation. He was a lot of things, but a good actor he was not. Still, Toggle didn't seem to notice. "Um, oh no, nothing I can share, I'm afraid." He gave her a small smile and then looked back down at his magazine. He knew how to close a conversation, that's for sure.

Toggle turned back to me, a furrow between her brows. "Well, I'm sure the person responsible will be found," she said. "Anyway, just wanted to say hi." She waved with one hand below her stack of books and headed toward the café.

As soon as she was out of earshot, "So we're pretty sure she came over just to ask you that question, right?"

"Probably," Jared said, "but way to go Magnum on getting the dirt on her residence."

I rolled my eyes. "Please, I do not have a Ferrarri or a moustache. I'm much more of a Columbo."

"People do underestimate you," he said as he leaned over and gave me a peck on the cheek. "I'm glad I'm past your bumbling ruse."

"Me, too," I said and settled back to read some more.

A FEW MINUTES LATER, the crew from the street fair came in, and Jared and I joined them over in the café after leaving our magazines and books on the library cart for someone to reshelve. "I want the full customer experience," I told Jared when he said he'd be happy to put them back.

Everyone was buzzing with energy when we sat down in the circle Dad had made from Rocky's chairs. Mom stood to debrief everyone. I looked over at Lu, and she just winked. Sometimes, the best thing to do when my mother was involved was to have no ego about your work. Clearly, Lu understood.

"Thank you, everyone, for all your hard work today." She glanced over at Lu. "And a special thanks to Lu Mason, our fearless leader."

Lu gave her a nod and shot me another wink. My mother also did not understand situational irony, apparently.

"I have not done the formal tally, but my quick count says we raised just over $1000 to support the St. Marin's Cat Colony."

"Oh, it has a name now," Henri said from her seat by her husband. "Fancy!"

"Well, we had to call it something," Pickle added. "Money for strays just doesn't have the same ring to it."

The group chuckled before Mom continued. "And that, of course, doesn't include the donations that will come in from the shop owners. I expect we may double that total."

Mart led us all in a small round of applause. "And how did the food and cooler donations go?"

Bear smiled. "Very good. We got over 40 coolers, and we gave most of them out already to residents." He turned to me. "If it's okay with you, Harvey, we told people they could get a cooler here over the weekend if they wanted one."

"Totally fine," I said. "I'll let everyone know."

"And we have about 200 cans and 25 bags of cat food. You should be set for a couple months, Sheriff," Pickle added.

Tuck smiled. "Excellent. Thank you all." He turned to Jared. "You don't mind if we store all of that in your office, do you?"

Another round of laughter passed through the room. "Actually," Cate said. "I was going to offer to keep the cat food at the co-op, kind of make it a permanent display in the lobby to encourage people to keep donating. Activist art, sort of," she said with a smile.

"Even better," Jared said loudly and received a chuckle for his quick response to defending his territory. "And maybe you can keep the coolers there, too? That way people can keep donating, and you can keep distributing. If you don't mind, Harvey."

"Not at all. Why don't we keep a couple here so that people

can get them if they come this weekend but send the rest with Cate for her installation," I added, happy to not have even more stuff in our backroom. "And maybe Marcus can do a display in one of our windows and use a bit of the food and a cooler to help with the continuing donation drive?"

"Good idea," Mom agreed. "I'll get the nonprofit status set up asap."

I looked at Lu again, and this time, she just rolled her eyes. Of course Mom would do that. Of course she would, Lu's face seemed to say, but not with any vitriol.

"Alrighty then," Mom said. "I think that concludes our business. If you all could help us tote coolers and food, that would be great. Then, everyone home to rest up. Our festivities start in earnest tomorrow."

"I thought they started yesterday with the shower," Lucas said into my ear as he passed, a witty but wise man not to say that to my mother.

I bumped him with my elbow and began putting the chairs back. "Um no," Elle said as she literally tugged a seat from my hands. "No work. None. Go home. Rest."

With a shake of my head, I thanked her, and then Jared and I waved to Marcus, hooked the two pooches to their leashes, and slipped out the back door to his truck. I had to admit, it felt kind of good to just leave everything to everyone else for a change. "Let's go home and eat popcorn and watch something stupid," I said after we'd lifted the basset and the hound, who feigned in ability to jump because her brother did, into the back seat.

"You read my mind." He started up the truck and drove us home.

THE NEXT MORNING, after watering all the potted plants to be sure they were healthy for tomorrow but that we didn't have puddles all over the porch and patio for the ceremony, I installed myself back in my reading chair and finished Pan's beautiful book and sad book. I suppose I could have chosen something super light and fun for the weekend of my wedding, but I found more serious fair, literary books, helped focus my mine when life threatened to be stressful. Pan's work certainly did that. I was going to be recommending it to everyone.

Jared had gone for a run – an activity I would never understand – and now that he was home and showered, we needed to get prepped for the rehearsal dinner proper. Max had offered to host it at Le Cuisine, and Jared's parents had been delighted with the idea. Despite that we were in our 40s and this was my second marriage, all the parental units had insisted on keeping the traditional rolls in terms of payment – so the _____ were covering the rehearsal and rehearsal dinner, and my parents were paying for the wedding. Jared and I had tried to take those expenses on ourselves, but we lost that fight early on.

And their desire to pay came, as was reasonable, with a desire to manage the details themselves. We'd told them our preferences in terms of Max's menu – "So much mushroom risotto," I'd insisted – and we stressed that we wanted everything to be fun and casual. Mom had balked a bit at the fact that we'd included "Dogs and children welcome," on our invitations because she was worried it would be disruptive. Then, Jared had pointed out that disruptive was kind of the point. She didn't like it, but she gave us that one.

The one thing she wouldn't give up, though, was the desire to have the rehearsal in mid-afternoon so that we could "test the light" for photos with the same sort of daylight we'd have at the 3pm ceremony the next day. No amount of suggesting weather interventions or work schedules would budge her from this stance, and so on this one, we caved and had to prep the house for everyone to arrive at 2pm. "You must have time to get everyone in place," Mom had said when she'd insisted everyone come an hour early.

Jared and I had decided to make the most of that hour when we had lots of help and ask people to assist in getting the backyard set for the ceremony. This request had then prompted Mart to suggest everyone come at Noon and that she and Symeon would provide lunch. So now, at 10am on the day before our wedding, we were hosting, in our own home, a party for 35 or so people. Twenty years ago, I would definitely have been completely stressed out by that fact, and that stress would have made me resentful of the work I had to do.

But now with more wisdom and more financial means, I had found my way around the stress and the resentment – I had hired cleaners and insisted that Mart have the lunch catered. We were not going to be making deli trays and vacuuming this weekend. Nope, the cleaning team who kept up my store so beautifully had been gracious enough to let me hire them to come and make the house shine. And at 11:30, sandwich trays from our local gas station deli – which had the best sandwiches around, everyone knew – would arrive along with drinks, chips, and their special cookies. No one, including my mother as best I could help it, was going to be stressed out this weekend.

For the time before everyone came, Jared and I reading our boxes with our gifts for our wedding party and put them in his truck. Then, we laid out outfits for the four of us – Mayhem was wearing a pink scarf this evening, and Taco had wedding antlers to sport. And then, with an hour to spare, we were ready.

"Let's walk in the garden, enjoy it before it becomes a stage," Jared said.

"Love that plan." I slipped on the rubber gardening shoes that Jared had gifted me for my birthday and headed outside. The air was cool, but the sun was rapidly warming the air. It was going to be a perfect afternoon, and the forecast for tomorrow was perfect. I never counted the weather chickens this close to the water, but it looked like everything would be ideal for an outdoor wedding.

And the garden, of course, looked stupendous. Jared had been cultivating this garden for years now, and it showed. The plants were mature and mostly perennials. We'd added a few impatiens and begonias for color, and since we'd been very attentive with cover cloth after we put the begonias in early, they were filled out and blooming with reds, oranges, and peaches.

We'd decided early on that our color for the wedding would be green, and because there are so many greens in any garden, we just went with various shades. Mom, after a small conniption fit, acquiesced, and I was so excited to see what the women in my party chose for their dresses since we had, also, let them choose the style they wore. We were well past the delusion that a traditional bridesmaid dress would ever be reworn, and so I told them to pick a green dress they loved and gave them each money to do so.

While I was ankle deep in the pachysandra hunting down rogue bits of ground ivy and clover, Jared's phone rang. He answered, and quickly, his tone went from relaxed to police. "I'll be there in five minutes."

I stood up with a handful of ivy in my hand. "Something happen?"

He nodded. "I have to go, Harvey," he said as he took long strides toward me. "I'm sorry." He gave me a soft kiss. "I'll be back as soon as I can."

I waved the ivy at him. "As long as you're back by the time Mom starts the rehearsal. I can cover for you until then, but there's no hope if you mess up Mom's plans." I tried to keep my tone light because I knew that this was part of the life of law enforcement and because I knew Jared felt guilty about it.

But as soon as he left the yard, I sat down in the grass and let myself be very sad for a long minute. It was the day before our wedding, and my fiancé had just left me without explanation. Rational me understood. The part of me that had been deprioritized in a profound way earlier in my life, she was devastated and terrified.

Eventually, though, I got up, finished weeding what most obviously needed it, and headed back inside to shower and get ready for my guests. But first, I texted Mart and let her know that Jared had been called away by work.

9

By the time I got out of the shower, Mart, Elle, Cate, and Henri were all in the living room with snacks just for me – chocolate covered peanuts and red licorice ropes – as well as all the things they'd promised to bring for our day of rehearsaling. I teared up again when I saw them, but they quickly hustled me back up to my room with the snacks and put me in a chair to look out at our beautiful back yard while they did a practice make-up session for the ceremony and then a full-on rehearsal make-up face for today.

Now, my friends are quite adequate with make-up, and since I almost never wore any, I had asked them to help me with mine for the wedding. Something simple, I'd told them. Something good for the pictures but that also doesn't make me look like a clown in person.

I had no idea that such a request was going to result in them undergoing a YouTube-led make-up course that would involve fake eyelashes, contouring, and some eyebrow gel stuff. But it did, and despite my worry about Jared and the lingering, low-level fear I had that he wasn't coming back, I found myself laughing as my friends made me first look a bit like a drag queen and then like an anime star, and then finally, like myself if I was going to star in my own book-related reality show on TV.

When I said that, Henri adopted her best game show host voice and said, "Today, On BookWorms for Bucks, Harvey Beckett will be attempting her longest marathon read without a pee break. She's going for three hours, folks. Yes, that's right three hours."

I laughed until I actually had to pee, and as I went to the bathroom, I shouted, "I said 'reality show,' not game show." And that broke the entire room into laughter. It was a good afternoon.

Finally, my make-up much more subdued but still lovely for the rehearsal luncheon, we all went back downstairs to get the food ready for everyone. The men arrived right on time, with Mom and Dad, and soon my house was full of people, people who loved me and loved Jared and who obviously had known in advance that he was out on call because they didn't ask me about him at all. I appreciated the text group in a way I never had before.

When Lu arrived about 1, after finishing up her lunch rush at the food truck, I was only momentarily surprised to see that Tuck wasn't with her. He was our officiant, so the fact that he wasn't going to make it to the rehearsal was a little upsetting. But she assured me that he would be here – with Jared – as soon as possible. "And besides," she added, "he's been practicing his role on me for weeks now. I"ll fill in for the rehearsal." She pulled a baseball cap out of her purse and slipped it over her long wavy hair. "See?" she said.

The image of my boho friend in a "Mel's Station" baseball cap brought the smile right back to my face. "It's a good look," I said. "Maybe you and Tuck could match."

"Don't you dare say such a thing," she said and pulled me

out into the yard to supervise the placing of the chairs for the ceremony.

I managed to keep my mood relatively light all through lunch and set-up, but by the time the rehearsal was scheduled to begin, I was a mess inside. I had managed to not cry, yet, but I was definitely close to it. "Where is he?" I said to Mart as she brought me a glass of sparkling water. She knew wine was not my best choice in my emotional state, obviously.

"I don't know, Harvey, but I'm sending Symeon and Luke to find him. They aren't in the wedding party, so they can go look around." She took a deep breath and then cleared her throat. "They'll find him."

She made her way across the lawn to Symeon, and even from where I stood, I could see she was angry. She made these chopping motions with her hands when her temper was up, and I was suddenly so grateful for her and the other women around me. They would always, always take my side, even when they understood both sides of a situation. I needed that, more than I had ever realized in my life.

Despite Lu's kind and funny offer to officiate, it wasn't like someone could stand in for the groom, so rather than start the rehearsal as intended, Mom suggested we finish up the favors for the reception the next day. As a joke, Jared and I had considered giving everyone Jordan almonds with our initials sprayed on them, both because we love those things and because, at our age, we'd likely be the cause of several rounds of extensive dental procedures. But instead, we'd settled on giving everyone a plant. A tiny, tiny plant, of course, but a living plant nonetheless.

Jared and I had cultivated the succulents from our own garden, pulling off chicks and stems whenever the plants he'd started years ago had extra growth. We'd potted them up in tiny terracotta pots that Cate painted with our initials for us. Then, Mom had taken them home to add ribbons and, as she said, her own special touch. What that special touch was I had no idea, but I was glad for something to do.

Mom had brought all the plants with her because she had intended to take them over to the reception site – the local VFW hall – after the rehearsal dinner, but instead, everyone carried the flats of adorable pots to our porch and began adding ribbon.

Then, Mom went around and placed a beautiful copper flower spike in each. "I had them made by a man named Bjorn Sorenson who lives over near Charlottesville." Each spike had a wire ring around a gemstone of some sort. Quart, amethyst, malakite, all kinds of stones native to our area. They were gorgeous and the perfect touch for our gifts.

"Thank you, Mom," I said as I hugged her between her rounds of the plants. They are amazing. Just perfect."

Mom smiled at me and then put her hands on my face. "He's coming back, Harvey."

My mother and I had not always had the closest relationship, and so for her to not only realize I was upset but to understand why, well, that broke me open into tears for the second time.

"I know, Mom. At least I think I know." I sniffled against her shoulder as she pulled me into the house and then into a big hug. "I know he had to go. I know life isn't fair. I know this," I waved my hand around in front of my face, "isn't really about him. But I just wanted this weekend to be perfect."

Mom hugged me again and then said, "You know what, it's not the weekend yet. We are going to hold the rehearsal until Jared and Tuck get back. Then we'll do a quick run-through and head to Max's. Only when that rehearsal starts is it officially your wedding weekend. You still have a shot at perfect."

. . .

THAT IS HOW, on the day before my wedding, almost everyone I loved in the world was taking a mixology course led by Stephen and Walter. My friends were becoming quite expert at this field, and they put on a true bartending show for us on a make-shift bar that Pickle and Bear made from two sawhorses and a piece of plywood that they found in the garage. First, they covered the basics – how to shake a martini shaker, how to properly pour, the right type and temperature of which glass for which drink.

Then, they got us drunk. Well, not completely drunk. But tipsy. Good and tipsy, as good friends who know that a little alcohol is a massive help for my mood can do. They kept making us all "test" their various drinks, and by the time Symeon and Luke returned with the news that Jared and Tuck were on their way, I was a little wobbly but in much better spirits, pun fully intended.

I wasn't, however, drunk enough to not feel the wash of relief that came over me when Jared walked into the backyard, where I had been installed into a lawnchair and was receiving the world's best foot massage from Bear. The man was a master.

I couldn't say whether I stayed in that chair getting my massage because it was just so good or because some wounded child part of me was being petulant, but it didn't matter to my fiancé. He came right to me, knelt down, and said, "I'm so sorry, Harvey. I know this was the worst thing for you. But I'm here. I will always be here."

All our friend stood around us, and the men were already nodding. But the women watched my face and only when I smiled and said, "I know" did the smiles reached their faces. I had good friends.

"Well, let's get this show on the road," Tuck said as he pulled a black ball cap that said, "Officiant" in white embroidery on the top. "Max has agreed to hold dinner exactly one hour, and we all know Max."

We did all know our friend Max, and within seconds, everyone was in their places at either the back of the yard or the front under the arbor covered in just flowering jasmine. I ran into the house, determined to let Jared have this rehearsed moment of seeing me for the first time, and when I did, Elle slipped a pair of heart antenna draped in a veil onto the top of my head and grinned. "Got to give him a show today, too," she said and kissed my cheek.

Then, as I watched, first Cate, then Henri, then Elle, then Mart made their way down the aisle ahead of me, and then as Pickle took my arm, I stepped into the yard and watched Jared double over in laughter. All was well.

As SEASONED WEDDING GOERS, all of us, we ran through the rehearsal at break-neck speed, partially because we were too tipsy still to really be serious but also because we knew that Max would not be happy if our risotto sat even one minute too long.

Then, as everyone reloaded the flats of plants into Mom and Dad's back seat and trunk, Jared and I snuck up to our room for just a minute. "Are you okay?" he asked as soon as he shut the door behind him.

"I am now," I said and gave him a hug. "Are you?"

"Yes, and tonight, I will tell you all about what happened, but now, if you can wait, I'd love to just enjoy this." He flipped one of the antenna still on my head.

"I like that plan," I said. "But do tell me something. Does all this have to do with Penelope's murder?"

Jared nodded. "Yes, it does." He kissed me then. "More later. We have to get the dogs ready for dinner."

"What are you talking about?" I said. "Max is not going to let those dogs in to his restaurant."

"Oh no, of course not. But they have other plans." He

winked at me and then tugged me into the hall, where Mart sat with Mayhem and Taco, both in bibs that said, "We love our owners."

"They're all set," Mart said. "And their servers await."

"What is going on?" I asked as Jared took the leashes in one hand and my hand in his other.

"Oh you'll see," he said as he shot Mart a wink.

As soon as we got downtown, I saw it. My store was bedecked in edison bulbs, more than we'd ever had before. The alley between the hardware store and mine was festooned with them, and a canopy of lights even extended out onto the sidewalk. But it was the display in the front window, opposite the cat display that Marcus had made to look like a giant cat face, whiskers and all, that made me gasp.

There, in the center of the window, were life-sizes cut-out of Jared and me surrounded by the most beautiful white scrim and fairy lights. At their feet, a beautifully hand-painted sign read, "Our boss is getting married. See you Monday."

"They closed the store?" I said looking at Jared.

"They did," he said. "As of 4pm today, All Booked Up is closed until Monday with the blessings of all your customers."

I looked over at my store again and saw Rocky and Marcus out front, two baskets in their arms. Rocky lifted her hand and waved us over. "These," she said when we made it up the block, "are for you."

There, in the baskets were dozens of envelopes addressed to Jared and me from all around the country. "We might have slipped a wedding notice in our last newsletter," Marcus said. "These are from your customers. I know you don't have time to read them now, but I wanted you to know that we didn't close for our two busiest days of the week without forethought."

I swallowed back tears. "Thank you so much," I said and hugged both them and the baskets.

"Now, if you'll excuse me," Marcus said, "I have the canine rehearsal dinner ready inside. I'll join you in just a moment at the restaurant."

As he walked away, I turned to Jared. "Mom thought of everything."

"Well, actually," he said as he pulled me into his side as we walked, "your dad thought about the dogs. Sidecar is waiting inside. He called it a 'play date.'"

"What has happened to my father?" I said with a laugh as we pulled open the door to LeCuisine and were greeted with cheers from our people. It felt amazing.

THE MEAL WAS, of course, amazing. Max had decided we'd eat family style, so he'd made a variety of dishes, including my favorite of his mushroom risotto, and so we all feasted and sampled and talked. In so many ways, it felt like a massive family reunion, except we didn't really need to be reunited.

But we did seem to need this – the chance to be together to celebrate something good, the chance to just relax and let ourselves be served just a little. Even Max sat down with us as his staff tended the kitchen and the table. The conversation was lively and the food delicious, and by the time dessert was served on platters with all of Max's offerings in multiples, we were all full of mirth and good food.

But then, as is the way with these things, the chatter lulled, and suddenly, the fact that a murder had happened just a few days before was there floating like a thought bubble above our heads. I tried for a moment to think of something to say to bring back the frivolity, but I knew it wouldn't work. You couldn't force something like joy. It had to just come.

So instead, I leaned over and whispered in Jared's ear. "Can you tell everyone what you were going to tell me later?"

He looked at me closely and then said, "Sure." He caught Tuck's eye, and silently, they made an agreement, or rather probably confirmed the agreement they'd made earlier in the day. "Everyone, Harvey and I are sensing that it might be a good time to let you all know what we can about the murder investigation."

Mom's eyes darted to mine, and I nodded. For once, she didn't object on the basis of appearances or how the day was supposed to go. This time, she nodded.

"Tragically, there was another murder this afternoon," Jared said.

The room grew entirely silent. Even the servers stopped clearing plates.

"What?!" I asked. "Who? Someone who knew Penelope?"

"Sadly, it was Annette Gooden," Jared said and lay his hand on my shoulder. "She was found at her trailer early this morning by a client.

I found that I could swallow or breathe really. So I put my head down on the table and listened.

Tuck said, "There were signs of a struggle. She fought hard. But she was, apparently, overcome."

I kept my forehead pushed against the tablecloth as I concentrated on the way the fabric felt to my skin.

"Who are your suspects?" Bear asked.

"We aren't revealing those at this time, but we are calling in reinforcements from Easton, especially since we have events this weekend that cannot be changed," Tuck continued. "They are working as we speak, and we hope to have more news by morning."

I sat stock still and let my brain slow until I could sit up. "We need to postpone the wedding." I was looking at Jared, but of course, everyone at the table heard me.

"We are not going to do that," Mart said. "No."

"That's right," Cate added. "No one is going to take this day away from you, too."

I sighed. "It's not that. It's just that I don't want the spector of murder hanging over our day." I kept my eyes on Jared. "I don't want you to feel distracted from either your job or our wedding."

Jared turned town me and put his forehead against mine, and I briefly wondered if he could feel the imprint of the table-cloth on my skin. "Harvey, I am not distracted. I am totally focused on you. But if you feel like we need to postpone so that these deaths don't cloud our day, I completely understand."

The room had gone very silent again. I didn't have the capacity at the moment to look at all my friends, so I just turned to face Mart.

She met my eyes and nodded. "Whatever you need, Harvey."

I closed my eyes and nodded. "I need to sleep on it." I was typically quite impulsive. Quick to decide things and then just deal with the consequences. But I'd been trying to deal with my own anxiety that made me push for resolution so fast. And this was one of those times when parts of my brain were pushing for something that all of me couldn't decide yet.

"That is an excellent plan," Lu said as she stood up. "We could probably all use some sleep."

"I will text everyone in the morning," Mart said. "Keep us all up to speed."

I smiled at her and then waved to everyone before letting Jared lead me next door to get the dogs.

For their part, they looked, indeed, like they'd had an epic playdate. All three of them were passed out on their sides in the front window, and if I wasn't mistaken, their bellies were protruding a bit more than usual. If I'd had any doubt they were exhausted, I would have known as soon as I stepped into the store. The three-pitched sound of snores filled the air. I almost hated to move them.

Briefly, I considered leaving them there for the night, letting them sleep off their play hangovers. But they'd probably get a little scared. And they'd probably need to use the bathroom. Mostly, though, I just wanted my dogs with me tonight. So we woke them up and walked behind them to get them actually moving.

As we headed out the door, Marcus came in. "I'll tidy up anything they messed and take Sidecar over to your parents." He hugged me briefly. "Talk to you tomorrow."

"Thanks, Marcus," I said and then followed the dogs out the door with Jared right behind me.

BACK AT HOME, the four of us got cozy in the living room. Jared lit a fire, more for ambiance than for warmth, and the dogs took to their beds in front of it. Jared and I got blankets and laid down on either end of the couch, our legs entwined.

I knew all the traditions about the night before the wedding, about the groom not seeing the bride, but tonight, I needed to be with him. . . . and I expected he needed to be with me. Life was a lot at the moment.

Finally, after we'd been cuddled up and silent for a long time, I said, "I don't know what to do."

"I know," he said. "It's a hard decision, and we can make it together if you want. But if you just need to make the call, I am happy whatever you decide."

I squeezed his leg with mine. "Thanks," I sighed. "I don't know if there is a good choice here." I looked up quickly at him. "I mean, of course marrying you is a great choice. But doing it tomorrow, I'm just not sure."

He nodded. "I totally get it. And I absolutely see your point of view. You can't be in my head and know that all I can think about is marrying you. You know I want to do my job well, so it's reasonable to be expect I'd be distracted."

I sighed. "I hear you when you say you're not, and I believe you. But my anxious brain doesn't. She's terrified that our special day will be ruined."

"Come here," Jared said, and I flilpped around to lay against his chest.

"That helps," I said. "You know what else might help?"

"What's that?"

"Are there any more details from today that you were going to tell me but didn't think you could tell everyone?" I pushed back and look at him. "I'm not prying. And I don't want you to compromise anything, including your relationship with Tuck." I put my head back over his heart. "I was just thinking that if there was more you could share, maybe, I don't know, maybe it would help."

Jared thought for a moment and then said, "Well, I didn't really want to talk about the means of the murder at dinner, but I can tell you. Do you want to know?"

I didn't really because I didn't want to picture Annette Gooden dead, and so far I'd been able to avoid that. But I also did want to know. I wanted to understand, and it always seemed like more information might bring more understanding. I nodded my head.

"She was stabbed," Jared said into my hair. "With a kitchen knife."

I tried not to let my brain go there, to not imagine the woman's body with a knife in it, and remarkably I mostly succeeded. "No finger prints or other evidence?"

Jared shook his head. "I can't tell you specifics, but no, no clear evidence to point to the murderer."

"It was her kitchen knife?" I asked, again careful not to picture things too specifically.

"It was. Seemed like someone just grabbed it off the counter."

"So not pre-meditated then? Like Penelope?" I remembered seeing the spa owner's body with the groom shears sticking out of it and shivered.

Jared hugged me tight. "It would seem like it, but that also seems like more than coincidence."

I nodded. It did seem like that, but who would have it out for two pet groomers? That just seemed like a strange population of people to have that much grievance with.

We lay silently for a few more minutes before Jared said. "Did that help?"

I sighed. "Not really, but now I really feel like I need to sleep on things. Are you ready for bed?"

"Yeah," he said. "Let's go up. I'll read a bit if you need to go to sleep right away."

"Are you kidding? And miss out on my last night of reading as a single woman? No way," I said as I pulled him off the couch. "Besides, I'm just to the steamiest part of *The Graham Effect*."

Jared rolled his eyes and led me to the stairs.

The last thing I saw before I flipped off the living room lights was our two dogs, peaceful and snoring again by the fire. So much peace there.

10

The next morning when I woke up from a surprisingly restful sleep, Jared was already out of my bed. My heart started thudding immediately as I wondered if he had been called away again for police business.

But then I heard the familiar sound of him singing "Can't Fight This Feeling" by Justin Timberlake and smelled the bacon, and I smiled. A quick look at the clock told me it was almost 8am, and I'd slept for 11 hours.

And it was my wedding day. No doubt about it. I was getting married today.

The rest had cleared my head and calmed my spirit, and I was bound and determined to not let some jerk ruin my wedding day. I had Jared, and we had our people . . . and it as going to be amazing.

Before I even got out of bed, I texted all our friends on our group thread, and when I heard Jared shout, "YES!" from downstairs, I knew he'd gotten the message, too. The next thing I knew, he was bounding into the room and leaping on the bed. "I get to marry you today," he said.

"I get to marry *you*," I replied.

And then, two dogs jumped into the bed – well, Taco jumped against the bed so Jared could lift him in – and the four of us cuddled with delight for a few minutes until I remembered something very crucial. "Aren't you cooking bacon?"

"Shoot," Jared said and sprinted back down the stairs.

Neither Jared nor I was, for whatever innate and intractable reason, unable to cook bacon without burning it. On the rare occasion that the food turned out slightly crispy but not charred, it was cause for celebration. That morning was not one of those occasions.

When the dogs and I followed him downstairs, a thin haze of bacon-scented smoke filled the air, and a charred batch sat on the peninsula. "We may not be able to salvage this one," Jared said as he set the pan to soak in the sink. "Want to go out for breakfast?"

"Yes, yes I do," I said. "But let's go to that little spot off 13 toward Princess Anne. I don't really want to spend this morning with anyone but you."

"Agreed," Jared said. "Do you want to wear real clothes or on the morning of your wedding would you prefer, 'the early morning college student look?'"

I glanced down at my thread-bare pajama pants and threw caution to the wind. "Pj pants, please."

"Excellent," he pulled our jackets off the hooks by the door. "Let's go."

A FEW MONTHS AGO, Jared and I had discovered this little place right off the highway that we loved for breakfast. It was a white clapboard building that could use a fresh coat of paint, and the only sign you had that it was actually functioning was a neon open sign in a corner window. But it was, as these places often are, the locals hang-out, and the omelettes there were amazing.

In time, we'd learned it was called Bessie's and was run by a woman named, of course, Bessie, whose oak-brown skin was so wrinkled that it could have been a topographic map of the Rockies. But Bessie's spine was straight and her legs spry, and she served every single customer that came into her restaurant every day of the week except Sundays. On Sundays, as one would expect, she was at church, "as the Good Lord intended," she always said.

We had tried to eat at Bessie's on a Saturday or two before, and we'd always decided against it because the line was so long and our time so short. But today, we had the time, and perhaps because we were later than usual, the line wasn't bad at all. We were at a corner table by the kitchen window in ten minutes.

The pace was still brisk inside, so Bessie gave us a quick wave as one of her "girls," as she called them, brought us waters and plastic covered menus. "Bessie will be right with you," the woman who was several decades beyond girlhood said as she turned back to the door.

Sure enough, two minutes later, Bessie was there, her apron starched and her hair twisted back into a bun. "What can I get you fine folks? Something special for the wedding day?"

How Bessie remembered the details of our lives I've never been able to understand. But she never forgot a customer's birthday or anniversary. She was a marvel.

"Yes, ma'am," I said with a bright smile. "No better way than to start our wedding day than here," I said.

She winked. "Bacon, cheddar omelette with homefries – no onions – wheat toast with lots of butter and coffee?"

I sighed. "That's it," I said as I slid my menu back over to her.

She recited Jared's favorite of sausage and gravy over biscuits and turned to the kitchen window behind us to deliver our order verbally to the cook staff.

"I do not know how she does that," I said to Jared as Bessie ran a soft hand over my shoulder as she passed back by. "I cannot remember my own order, much less anyone else's."

Jared laughed. "But you do remember everyone's favorite books, right? Same thing."

I shrugged and smiled. "Maybe."

Our coffee arrived courtesy of another of the "girls," and we were chatting about the day ahead – how many times my mom would tell everyone to "take a deep breath" and how many glasses of wine Mart would try to slip me to help me deal with my mom – when the door opened, and we saw Caro and Sheila from the dog spa come in and slide into the booth closest to the door.

I started to wave but then decided I wasn't really in the mood to talk about Penelope or anyone else today, and I certainly didn't want my police officer husband to get derailed into work on our wedding day. "Let's just leave them be," I said as he turned to look at me.

"My thoughts exactly," He said and picked up my hand to kiss it.

Just then, though, Dr. Stoltzfus came in and was waved immediately over by the two young women in the booth. "Oh," I said, and Jared followed my gaze.

"Well, that is interesting," he said.

I nodded and slid my chair quietly around the table so my back was to their booth and my body partially blocking Jared, now across from me. "Holy cow," I said. "We do not think this is a coincidence, do we?" I hissed at my fiancé across the table.

"No, of course not, but if you think sounding like a member of Slytherin is going to keep our presence quiet, you might reconsider. Hufflepuff is more the vibe here," Jared said with a grin.

"I'm not feeling very happy go lucky right now," I said with a sigh. "what in the world could the three of them have to talk about?"

"You mean besides the murder of two of their rivals?" Jared gave me a wide-eyed look. "I have no idea."

I, unlike my best friend, was not a big conspiracy theorist. Mart could see a scheme in the way the soda guy restocked the shelves at the grocery store if you gave her a chance. I, however, usually trusted people too much. I wasn't prone to scheming, so I assumed the world wasn't either. But now, I was feeling very much like I needed to rewatch the X-Files and brush up on ability to identify collusion. "You don't think they were all in on it?" I said to Jared after one of the girls dropped off our breakfast.

He shrugged. "I have no idea," he carefully gathered a forkful of sausage, gravey, and biscuit. "But that is odd."

"Odd doesn't begin to cover it," I said even as I knew I shouldn't be getting so excited about it. "Do you think we could get Bessie or one of her girls to plant a bug a something?"

Jared almost spit out his mouthful of food. "First of all, Harvey, we are not bugging anyone's table at breakfast on our wedding day."

"And second of all?" I said with one eyebrow raised.

"I don't just carry surveillance equipment with me."

"Maybe you should?" I said a little more seriously than I intended.

Jared frowned. "Can you let this go, Harvey? I want to solve these murders as much as you do, but today is not the day."

I sighed and nodded. "You're right. But you'll at least tell Tuck what we're seeing."

He swallowed and took out his phone. "I'll do it right now." He tapped out a quick text and then said, "Now, can we eat and talk about who is going to cry the most at the ceremony?"

I smiled and tried my best to turn my focus totally toward my fiancé, who had placed his tears bet on Pickle but had my dad as a close runner up. But despite my best efforts, I could feel my imaginary antenna turning backward, straining to hear what the trio at the table across the room were saying.

I startled back to our table as Jared said, "Harvey," and put his hand on mine. "You are not the Bionic Woman. You cannot hear what they are saying."

I blushed. "That obvious, huh?"

"Well, I know you, for one. But also, you're leaning back so far that your chair might tip over." He chuckled as I let the front legs of the chair drop back to the ground. "I must say, though, despite your distraction, you made a good dent in your breakfast."

I looked down to discover that I had eaten almost everything on my plate, including two full pieces of toast, without remembering most of it. "Man," I said with a sigh, "I don't even remember tasting it."

Jared laughed. "Well, that will be punishment enough. The cooks are on point today."

"Crap," I said. "Well, that'll show me."

Jared's phone vibrated on the table, and he tapped the screen to show the notification. "Tuck says he'll have the deputy from Easton follow up." He turned the screen to me. "Let it go, Harvey," the message said.

"I feel so seen," I said with a laugh. "Let's go. Maybe if we get out of here, I won't be so distracted." I took his hand. "I don't want to be distracted," I said quietly into his ear as we headed toward the register.

"I know," he said before kissing my cheek and then waving, very pointedly, toward the booth by the door. "It's one of the things I love about you."

I stared at him and will myself not to look back at the three people by the door. "You want them to know we saw them?"

"Oh definitely. When people get flustered, they make mistakes." Jared took out his wallet and paid our bill. "Your turn?" he whispered as we headed for the door.

This time, I put on my brightest smile and waved at the vet and the two spa employees, and when I did, I saw what Jared meant – all of them looked mortified.

AS WE DROVE BACK to St. Marin's, I let my mind spin for a bit about what we'd just seen. The sun was out, and the breeze was light, so I lay my head back against the doorframe and imagined. Could Sheila, Caro, and Dr. Stoltzfus been scheming to take over the entire pet market in St. Marin's? Did they knock off Penelope and Annette to narrow their competition? Was there some sort of takeover plan underfoot?

My wild mafia-style pet conspiracies made me giggle, and Jared looked over with a smile. "What is going on in that beautiful brain of yours, Harvey?"

I smiled and said, "Have you seen the movie *Cats and Dogs*?"

"I'm sad to say I haven't had the pleasure," he replied. "Please fill me in."

I told my fiancé about the children's movie where dogs and cats are in battle to control the world whilst leaving the humans to believe we still ran things. "I just had this vision of the three of them as covert agents for the cat contingent, trying to seize control of our town."

Jared was quiet for a minute. "But there's a flaw in your plan – Caro and Sheila primarily work on dogs." He looked at me out of the corner of the eye. "Could it be that the cats and dogs are now working together?"

The two of us fleshed out our theory that the pets were taking over until we were crying with laughter. "Gives a whole new meaning to the phrase 'Animal Control,'" Jared said as we parked at our house.

"Thank you," I said as he opened my truck door. "I needed that."

He tugged me against his chest. "Me, too," he said as he

kissed my hair. "Now, let's be serious for a minute." He stared intently into my eyes. "Are you willing to be Mayhem's servant, for a time, if need be? Will you go undercover for the human cause?"

"Only if you'll answer to Taco?" I said as I tried to press the smile out of my lips.

"Easy," Jared said as he led me toward the house. "He'll just have me bring him food and lift him onto things so he can see or sleep. I'm up for that."

We were still laughing as we walked into our house to find Mom and Mart teetering on our dining room chairs as Elle directed them in how to hang the swag of greenery and flowers that she had created for us.

"Stop," Jared said firmly as he entered the room. "We will not have any broken bones today." He helped Mom off her chair as Symeon stepped up and got Mart down.

I looked at the beautiful, long swatch of magnolia, holly, and cedar swags that Elle had decorated with tulip, daffodil, and rose blossoms. "Wow," I whispered. "This is beautiful."

"Yes, it is," my mom snapped, "but we can't get it to stay up across this space." She gestured across the wide archway that crossed from our dining room to the kitchen. "We've been at this for 30 minutes, and I must move on to the chair swags."

"You go do those," I said to Mom. "Let Mart and I take care of this," I pointed toward the now dropping array of plants at our feet.

"No, Harv—," Mom started to say.

I cut her off. "Mom, I need to stay busy. I've got this."

She stared at me a minute and then gave a curt nod before going out the backdoor with a shout at the poor soul about to have all their work on the chair swags redone.

"Let's put this outside," I said to Mart. "No one will be coming through here anyway."

She smiled and picked up the other end of the long line of

greenery. "I might have said that to your mom," she said as we went out the front door and down the sideyard. "I didn't want to upset the mother of the bride."

I laughed. "You're a good woman, but nothing is going to keep my mother from getting worked up today. It's just her way." I stopped at a point about two-thirds of the way to the backyard and looked over my shoulder to see Elle trailing behind us with a handful of ribbons and florist wire. "This look good?" I said.

"Just what we talked about," Elle said as Symeon set up a ladder next to Mart and then climbed it before following Elle's directions on how to get the arch to say in place.

Ten minutes later, and we had a gorgeous, natural entry way from the sideyard into our ceremony space. Elle and I had discussed this plan, the way I wanted people to feel like they'd gone through a portal to the wedding, and this was perfect. "I love it," I told my flower farmer friend. "Thank you."

She kissed my cheek and then dashed through the arch. "Better go see how those chair decorations are coming along?"

"Let me know if you need champagne for fortification?" I shouted as she disappeared around the corner. "Speaking of which?" I raised my eyebrows to the maid of honor.

"I've got you," Mart said as she took my hand and pulled me back into the house. As we jogged through the living room, I saw Jared and Tuck talking in the corner, but Mart didn't give me a chance to stop before she had a champagne glass in my hand and was pulling me upstairs to our bedroom. "No more seeing your fiancé today. I've allowed you enough time to flaut the rules of wedding luck. He can see you when you come down the aisle."

I started to protest, but then I looked carefully at my best friend. She looked near tears. "Oh Mart," I said. "What's wrong?"

"Not a thing," she said. "I mean, nothing's wrong. It's just that. Well, I'm going to miss you." A single tear slipped down her cheek.

"What in the world?" I said as I tugged her down on the bed next to me. "I'm not going anywhere. What are you talking about?"

"I know, but when people get married, things change. Don't you remember how it was when we were in our 20s. People get married. Then they move or have kids, and suddenly, you're not as close anymore."

I did remember that, and I did remember how painful it had been. "Mart, oh, friend, it's not going to be like that for us. We aren't 20-somethings who are still figuring out who we are in the world. We're full-grown women with our careers and lives we love here, in St. Marin's. I'm not moving, and Lord knows I'm not having kids."

"Me neither," she said with a choke. "Are you sure?"

"Woman, have you seen that store I own? If you think I'm giving that up anytime soon, you are delusional." I met her gaze and smiled. "And if you think this 48-year-old body is going to decide to procreate, you are in need of a serious reality check."

She smiled, just a bit.

"Can you see me pregnant? My hips don't really want me to get up off the floor now as they are. If I tried to push a child through them, my SI joints would never recover. I'd have to constantly scout for chairs and cars that didn't require me to lower my hips below my knees." I laughed. "I'm not living like that."

At this, Mart's face broke into a wide smile. "You have a point, and my knees aren't any good at hauling you up either." She wiped her face. "Thank you for letting me having a breakdown on your wedding day."

"Of course," I said as I hugged her one more time. "Alright, now where is everyone else?"

As if they had been waiting outside the door, which they

probably had, Henri, Elle, and Cate came bustling in with clothing bags and make-up pouches and more wine.

"You ready?" Cate said as she looked at me. "You've eaten?"

I nodded. "Yes," I said and started to fill them in on who we'd seen at Bessie's but decided against it. This was my time with my best friends. I was going to focus on that. "Too much probably," I said instead. "But I am good to go until the reception."

"Well, just in case," Cate said as she pulled out a canvas tote, "I have trail mix, licorice ropes, seltzer water, regular water, and a whole jar of peanut butter and a spoon."

"You have thought of everything," I said with a laugh and then sighed. "Pass me the peanut butter."

For the next hour, my friends did my hair, plied with me with just enough wine to keep me limber but not tipsy, and applied my make-up until I felt like, probably for the first time in my life, that I finally had the girls I'd wished I'd had when I was a teen. The ones would come when I called with the code word for crisis, the ones who would fawn over the latest boy with me, the ones who would stay up all night talking with me about life and dreams and how exactly Molly Ringwold got her hair to do that. Our worries were a bit heavier than in my teen years, but these were those friends.

Soon enough, it was time for all of us to change, and I waited, sipping some of Cate's seltzer water while each of them slipped into their green dresses. I'd recently read a great romantic comedy, *The Unhoneymooners*, where the bridesmaids were dressed in green and looked, as one character said, like green Skittles. But my women had chosen their shades more thoughtfully, and they each looked radiant.

Henri was in a sheath of emerald satin covered in a sheer overlay that hugged all her curves but somehow also flowed beautifully around her. She pinned her braids up with sprigs of eucalyptus and baby's breath that Elle had brought for everyone, and she looked magical.

Cate was in a baby doll dress of pale green, somewhere between mint and lime and not at all the color of hospital walls, as I had feared it might be. She skirt hit her just above her knees, and she had found strappy, low heels that looked perfect. The flowers in her hair were attached to a small clip that she wore on one side.

Elle had donned a linen dress with an empire waist in an forest green that brought out the green flecks in her golden eyes. She had made herself a wreath of flowers for her blonde curls, and even though she was the oldest among us, she looked, somehow, the most youthful in her simplicity.

And Mart had chosen a silk trouser suit in a shade of green that tilted almost brown in some lights. The legs on her pants flowed around her like a skirt, and the fitted suit jacket gave her a polished yet whimsical look that was just her personality. She had pulled her hair into a French twist, and Elle wove flowers through the back of her head.

While I'd heard a little about what each of my bridesmaid's dresses was going to look like, I had been very quiet about my own dress, letting my mom and Mart be the only ones with me when I found it. Now, though, as I slid satin drape up over my body, everyone gasped. The dress itself was very simple – off-white satin that hung straight from my shoulders. No sleeves, and a scooped collar.

But the magic was that it was hand-stitched with tiny flowers in bright colors all over it. "Harvey," Henri said after Mart finished zipping up the back, "I can't imagine a more fitting dress for you in all the world."

Then, my friends were gathered around me in a hug so tight that we all had to straighten hair and reapply make-up before we were ready to go.

And then, it was time. Mom came in and pretended like she

didn't want to cry, and Dad joined us and didn't even pretend. Then, we heard the music start below, and the procession began.

Jared was as handsome as ever in his dark gray suit, and when he saw me, tears sprang to his eyes and he held very, very still. Then, when I reached him and he took my hand, he leaned over and whispered, "How did I ever get so lucky?"

The rest of the ceremony was a blur as Tuck, in a seer sucker suit that only a Southern man can pull off, led us through our vows and then pronounced us husband and wife. It was simple, elegant, and short, and soon, I was married and going back down the aisle with my husband as all the people we loved hooted and hollered like they were at the state fair pig races. It was perfect.

After we had pictures taken and reconvened at the VFW hall, the crowd was well-behaved but at the edge of raucous, especially with the pack of dogs that had gathered and was roaming, as a coordinated unit, beneath the tables in the hopes of dropped snacks.

We did all the usual wedding things – but our way of course – and Jared and I opted to sit at a table up front alone with beds for Taco and Mayhem in front of us. The dogs, however, were not so inclined to stay put, so we bribed them into their places just long enough for a photo and then left them to roam while the rest of us ate and cut cake and then danced the night away.

There's something magical about the dancing at a wedding. Some people are stellar at it, having perfected The Wobble at many an affair, but most of us are just messy and slightly unco-ordinated but gleeful. There aren't many times in adult life when glee is the pervading emotion in a room, but weddings brought that out. And I was immensely glad ours did.

Five hours after it all began, the party finally wound down, and the only two people left on the dance floor were our friend Woody's granddaughters, who had fallen asleep in a pile right in the middle. I felt like I could join them, but I didn't relish what it would be like to get up off the floor later. So I contented myself with a chair by the door to wish everyone well.

"Are you glad we didn't do the big birdseed sendoff thing?" Jared said as some of the last guests got into their cars and honked as they drove away.

"I am. Younger Harvey would have enjoyed the big fanfare, but now, I like being the one to send people home. Maybe it's my age, but that feels like my roll now – to do what I can to help the people I love be okay." I looked around the room at my friends who were just as exhausted as I was but were, still, cleaning up from the party. We'd all come the next morning and do the deep clean, so for now, they were just making sure no food was left out.

Henri walked over with a mound of something so thoroughly covered in plastic wrap that it would probably survive into the next millinia. "The top of your wedding cake," she said as she handed it to Jared. "I did my best to prevent freezer burn, but don't plan to eat more than one bite next year."

"Noted," Jared said as she stood up. "You guys got this?" He asked Henri.

"Yes, absolutely. You two go. We'll see you in the morning for breakfast and gifts."

The stack of gifts was enormous, and there was no way I was up for loading those things let alone opening them. "Great," I said as I hugged her. "See you then."

Jared whistled his standard call for the dogs, and I stood, waiting for them to join us so we could all go home and sleep.

But they didn't come. Jared whistled again, and still no dogs.

I called out to them, and when they still didn't emerge from where they were sleeping, all of us began a methodical search under table clothes to see where they might be.

Twenty minutes later, though, and the dogs were nowhere to be seen. Of course people had been in and out of the hall all night, so it was possible that the dogs had slipped out. But given that Sidecar and Sasquatch were still there, sound asleep by the kitchen les any treat fall astray, it wasn't likely that our two had just run off. Plus, just to allay my fears about that possibility, Dad had bought both of our dogs GPS collars and set up a perimeter fence around the hall just for tonight. He had his smartwatch set to get alerts if they crossed the boundaries, but nothing had pinged.

The collars, though, were helpful because they told us the location of the dogs, and when we saw the two blue dotes on the app's map, Jared and I bolted over to the corner of the lot near a stand of pines, expecting to find our silly, sleepy dogs there. Instead, all we found were their collars.

Someone had dognapped Mayhem and Taco.

11

I am not someone who treats my pets as I would human children, if I had any, but to say I was bereft that my dogs had been taken was an understatement. That they had been taken on my wedding night felt the largest possible injury I could imagine someone could inflict on me short of harming the people I loved.

Blessedly, everyone in St. Marin's knew that and so as Tuck put out the word that Taco and Mayhem had been abducted, everyone went to work looking. Since the dogs were both incapable and too lazy to have slipped out of the collars themselves, we went on the presumption that someone had driven away with them. And while a few people came right away to the VFW hall to scour the grounds and nearby farmland, most folks took to their cars and began looking for the dogs, calling their names, and keeping their eyes out for anyone with a basset hound and a black mouth cur.

"I'm not sure who was stupid enough to take *your* dogs, Harvey," Lucas said, "but they won't be missing long."

I wanted to believe him, to have faith that their presence in the store window on so many days had made them completely recognizable to almost everyone, that someone would spot them soon and bring them home to us. But a cold chill in the bottom of my stomach told me that this wasn't going to be so easy. If someone had the gall to steal my dogs from my wedding reception, then they weren't about to be lax about having them in public.

EVERYONE GATHERED at our house to make a plan as soon as the hall was locked up and the APB – All Pooches Bulletin, as Tuck called it in a sweet attempt to lighten the mood – was issued. Mart brewed strong coffee, and Cate wrangled lots of snacks for everyone. We were all dragging after a long day, but I knew our friends were as committed to finding our dogs as we were.

Jared and Bear headed out as soon as they had changed to use Jared's patrol car light to spot around town and then in widening circles just in case someone had taken the dogs and then let them off just to scare us.

Tuck, Lu, Mom, and Dad had started a phone tree of sorts and were sending texts or making calls to everyone in town to let them know the dogs were missing and to ask people to let them know if they saw them.

"Reminds me," Elle said, "of those prayer chains my mom used to do when I was a kid. Everyone would have two or three people to call to ask them to pray for who or what needed it. It worked really well." She put her hand on mine, where it rested on our dining table. "It will work now."

I nodded, trying to be positive but also needed to reserve my energy to stave off the panic attack I could feel threatening at the back of my head. I kept reminding myself that I was safe, that the dogs were likely safe, that everyone I loved was helping.

But no matter what I told myself, I couldn't seem to calm down. By the time Stephen came over, knelt beside me, and handed me two blue capsules, I was having trouble breathing. "Harvey, you trust us, right?" he said as he pressed the pills into my hand.

I nodded, unable to speak. I did trust them.

"Then take those and go to bed. We will get you if we hear anything." He held out his hand, and when I took it, he tugged me gently to my feet.

Mart put her arm around my waist and led me upstairs. I wanted to protest, to say that I needed to stay, that my dogs needed me. But I'd finally learned that I wasn't nearly as essential to most anything as I had once thought I was. And what I needed now was rest and to trust my friends. So when Mart handed me a glass of water, I swallowed the pills and climbed into bed.

The last thing I remember from that night was Mart hanging up on my wedding dress and telling me she loved me.

THROUGH THE MAGIC of sleep aids, the next few hours passed without my knowing, and when Jared's familiar hand gently shook me awake, I felt much calmer, if quite groggy. "Galen has a lead," he said.

It took my brain a few minutes to catch up and figure out, first, who Galen was, and then, what he had a lead about. But as soon as I put all the pieces together, I jogged downstairs in my Winnie the pooh pjs to get all the details.

Everyone was still there. Cate and Elle were sleeping on the touch, and Symeon had taken one of the club chairs and was snoring. My other friends looked like they might have caught a nap at some point too if hair was an indicator, but now, most everyone was wide awake and gathered around Tuck at the table. "What's happening?" I asked.

"Galen was just telling us what came through on his Instagram feed," Mart said as she stood up and let me sit down next to Tuck in her seat. "Galen, would you mind telling Harvey?"

"Hi Galen," I said as I realized our friend was on the Tuck's phone screen. "Sorry to keep you awake so late."

He waved a hand. "I don't sleep much at night anyway. So I put Mayhem and Taco's pictures up on my feed and asked people to let me know if they saw their doppelgangers."

When I frowned in confusion, Tuck turned to me and said, "I didn't want a bunch of good intentioned people trying to rescue the dogs themselves."

I was still a little groggy, but then it clicked. "So you made it a kind of contest. Who could find a pair of dogs like ours?" I smiled. "That's a good idea."

"It was actually Galen's," Henri said. "Social media wizard."

"never mind that," Galen said. "Someone in Easton took a picture. Show her."

Mart held her screen out for me to look at and there were my dogs in the front seat of what looked like a gray sedan of some sort. They were gazing out the window, and while they didn't look to be in distress, I could tell from the way that they were panting that they were either immensely hot – unlikely at night in April – or scared. "Where was this?"

"By the movie theater," Bear said. "Jared and I are on our way there. Do you want to come?"

I was already on my feet. "How long ago?"

"15 minutes," Galen said as Tuck followed behind us.

"Meet us there," Tuck said. "We're all going."

Never in the many times that I had entangled myself in one of Tuck's investigations had he ever said it was a good idea for all of us to go anywhere in pursuit of a case. So I was puzzled by this declaration, but I didn't question it. I wanted all the help I could get to get our dogs back.

Jared and I took his truck with Mart and Symeon squeezed into the back seat, and everyone else, including the very groggy

Cate and Elle, piled into cars as we caravanned out of St. Marin's and up the road to the larger town of Easton. Normally, I enjoyed the 15 minute ride with it's glimpses of the water and the agriculture along the way. That night, though, I just wanted to get there.

"Can't we go any faster?" I asked my husband – jarring myself with that thought.

"Not if we want to arrive without fanfare," he said and put his hand on my leg. "I have my light," he said as he gently kicked the blue removable sphere that he kept beneath his driver's seat. "But probably better for us not to roll up with lights flashing, right?"

I sighed and nodded. "Right, and if five cars peel into the parking lot, we might as well add sirens," I said.

He smiled over at me. "Call Tuck will you?"

I took Jared's phone from the seat beside him and dialed his boss's number. "What's the plan?" my husband asked after I put the phone on speaker and placed it on his holder in the dash.

"You guys pull in," Tuck said. "A new showing begins in 15, so it'll seem normal. Elle, Pickle, Bear, and Henri will park, too."

"Understood," Jared said. "The rest of you?"

"We're going to fan out across the area and be near all the parking lot exits just in case." Tuck sounded stern. "But apart from me, no one else can stop a vehicle, Harvey."

I was a bit startled by the statement directed at me. "Okay, right?"

"But we can follow, so if necessary, that's what we'll do." He sighed. "Back up is on the way, too."

For a minute, I tried to think of what other friends might be joining his ramshackle task force and then suddenly realized that Tuck meant other actual police officers. "Okay," I said quietly before Tuck hung up.

I forced myself not to ask the thousands of questions spinning through my head. Instead, I took a deep breath and closed my eyes for a moment.

"You okay?" Jared said as he slid his hand over mine.

I nodded. "You know not really, but yes, given the situation, yes." I squeezed his fingers.

"It's going to be okay," he said.

"You promise?"

He smiled, but I noted that he didn't answer me.

WE FINISHED the ride in silence, which was just as well because it was taking all of my concentration to just breath and not slide into panic. When I saw the shopping center with the movie theater come into view ahead, I swallowed hard, took another deep breath, and then did what Jared had said he did every time he was on duty – I pushed all my emotions into a little ball behind my sternum and focused on the details around me.

In the side mirror, I saw Tuck and Lu's car turn off just before we got to the light at the shopping center, and I watched as Stephen and Walter's vehicle pulled into the shopping center behind us but then turned left when we went right. Bear's car followed us into the lot but then parked a few rows away, and I saw Cate and Lucas's SUV and then Symeon's truck on the far end of the shopping center lot. We were all in place.

"According to the report Galen got," Jared said as he and I stepped out of the car and headed toward the movie theater, "was of a gray sedan. So keep your eyes peeled. Casually." He squeezed my hand.

I looked around like I was just taking in the weather or something. For the life of me I couldn't remember what I actually did when I walked across a parking lot. Did I look around? Did I look at the ground? Did I stare straight ahead? I had no idea how to be casual.

But then, from around the side of the theater building, I

heard a familiar sound: Mayhem's bark. Her voice was usually like nails on a chalkboard to me because of the pitch and volume, but now it sounded like music. "There," I said and pointed.

Jared had heard her, too, and we were both sprinting toward the sound before I could even tell my body to do it. I heard lots of footfalls behind us and hoped it was our friends coming up in support and not the dognappers. But even it was the bad guys, I wasn't stopping. I could hear her, and she was scared.

As soon as I rounded the corner of the building, I saw my dogs tied to a pipe halfway down the building. Jared was much faster than I was, and he had almost reached them. But he stopped a few feet short.

"What are you doing?" I shouted as I ran up beside him and collided with his outstretched arm.

"We need to be sure the scene is clear, Harvey," he said. "We don't want anyone to get hurt." He turned and looked at me, holding my ees until I nodded that I understood.

"You think there's a bomb? A trip wire? A mine?"

This made him laugh out loud. "No, nothing like that. I wouldn't have come down here, or more importantly, let you come if I thought there was any immediate danger." He hugged me. "We just don't want to disturb any evidence."

I chuckled at myself, but my bit of humor didn't last long because now not only was Mayhem barking but Taco had started his hound-dog yodel. It was so loud in the small alley between the concrete buildings that I wanted to put my hands over my ears.

Instead, though, I sat down on the ground and said, "It's okay, pups. We'll be there in just a minute. It's okay."

Meanwhile, Jared turned to Henri, Bear, Pickle, and Elle behind us and said, "Please go get Tuck." Then, he took out his phone and took photos of everything, getting close every few minutes until he was able to put a calming hand on each of our dog's heads. Only then, did they settle all the way and wag their tails.

"Harvey, I'm going to release them from the pipe. Catch them, will you?" Jared said as he bent down and quickly unwrapped first Mayhem and then Taco and let them come to me.

As soon as they were close, I kissed their faces, and with Henri and Elle's help, checked them over to be sure they weren't hurt. We didn't find any cuts or scrapes, and they didn't seem to be groggy or anything like they'd been drugged. Still, I was having our vet check them over completely first thing Monday.

Since Mom and Dad had stayed at our house just in case someone called or came by with info about the dogs, Henri quickly texted them to let them know we'd found the pups. Then, she let Galen know too, even as all our other friends crowded into the thing alleyway. "Where were they?" Stephen asked as he sat down cross-legged on the dirty pavement and pulled all 80 pounds of Taco into his lap.

"Tied to that pipe-thingy," I said before studying the pipe in question. It was silver and about two inches around, came up out of the ground, had a short section perpendicular to the ground with a dial on it, and then went back underground again.

"Good thing it's sturdy," Walter said as he knelt down and scratched Mayhem's head as she leaned against me. "That's a gas pipe. If they had pulled too hard, they might have caused it to leak or even come lose altogether."

Stephen shot his husband a strongly worded look of warning, and Walter promptly turned to me. "But those things are really sturdy. Even these two wild things couldn't have pulled it loose. I'm just thinking with my contractor brain. Sorry."

He stood up and wandered over to where Lucas, Cate, and Henri were talking nearby as I returned my eyes to the pipe, grateful that my dogs hadn't pulled their full power into getting free. That could have killed them and everyone in the theater, too, if what I knew of gas leaks and explosions was correct.

"You are doing great, aren't you?" Stephen said as if talking to an infant but facing Taco. "Maybe it was even worth it to be dognapped just to get this kind of attention."

I looked at Taco's relaxed, droopy face and thought Stephen probably wasn't wrong. From that dog's point of view, the excitement had been well worth it. But against my body, I could feel that Mayhem was still shaking and quickly waved for Elle to come over. "In Jared's truck, under the back seat, there's a blanket. Could you get it?"

"Of course," Elle said. "You cold?"

"Not me." I tilted my head toward Mayhem. "She's terrified."

What I really wanted to do was gather my dogs and husband into our truck and go back to our house, where we could all get into bed with our favorite snacks before snuggling up to go to sleep. But this was a crime scene, and I knew I wasn't going to be allowed to take the victims away until the police had thoroughly checked the scene. I just hoped that didn't take long.

"CAN I GET YOU A COFFEE?," a woman said over my shoulder as I sat, a few minutes later, snuggling Mayhem against me in her blanket.

I looked up to see Rocky smiling at me. "Woman, you don't have to get me coffee?" I said with a smile. "What are you doing here?"

"Are you kidding?" Rocky said. "We came as soon as we could."

Rocky and her fiancé Marcus had been at the wedding, of course, but since the store was going to be closed the next day, they had left a couple of hours before the rest of us so they could get a good night's sleep.

"You didn't have to do that," I said as I gestured at the rather large entourage now crowded into the tiny alley.

"Of course we didn't have to, but we wanted to." She smiled at me and then sat down and began rubbing Mayhem's back, too. "They're okay, right?"

I nodded. "This girl is still scared, but once we get her home, she'll be fine."

"Actually, about that," Marcus said as he walked over with Jared at his side. "Why don't we take them with us for the night? That way, you don't have to worry about them, and you can come get them tomorrow or just pick them up from the shop on Monday if you want."

Jared nodded. "I think that's a good idea, Harvey." He bent down to rub Mayhem's shivering head. "We're going to be here a bit longer, and both of us could use the peace of mind that these two are safe and secure in an "undisclosed location.'"

He was smiling, but I knew he was actually dead serious. The policeofficer concern was there in his eyes. "Okay," I said, "if you two don't mind. You have food and such?"

"Already taken care of," Cate said as she took Mayhem's leash from my hand. "Lucas is going to get their favorite, and we'll meet them at Marcus's place. Okay?" She looked at me until I nodded.

"Thank you," I said.

"No problem," Rocky said as she stood up and then hugged my shoulders. "I'm thinking we might take Sasquatch and Side-car, too, make it a doggy slumber party."

Cate clapped. "Oh, Sas would love that. I'll have Lucas grab him on the way."

Stephen scooted over to sit next to me under Mayhem's blanket as Taco and Mayhem trotted along willingly behind

Cate and then began to wag their tails vociferously when they reached where Mom and Dad were standing with Sidecar.

"They do not know what they're getting into," Stephen said.

"Normally, I'd agree, but there's been so much excitement today, I think our two will probably crash out." I glanced at him out of the corner of my eye. "After conning Rocky and Marcus into giving them as many treats as their puppy dog eyes can acquire."

"That sounds about right," he said and then leaned against me, much as Mayhem had done, but this time, it was for my comfort, not his.

WE ENDED up being in the alley for another half-hour or so while Tuck, Jared, and a handful of uniformed officers from Easton did a thorough scan of the area and talked with the movie theater and other local store employees. One ticket taker remembered seeing someone who he thought was a man take the dogs down the alley, but he hadn't paid much attention because unfortunately, this alley was used by animals, and a few humans, as a bathroom quite often.

From him, though, we learned that this occurred just before the 9pm showing of the latest Brendan Frasier movie, which meant the dogs hadn't been missing from the VFW hall for more than about 45 minutes when we discovered they were gone. Unfortunately, that also meant that most of our guests had already been gone by that point, so we had fewer people to ask about who might have seen someone with Mayhem and Taco.

"It's feeling very much one step forward, two steps back," I said to Jared as we climbed back into his truck and headed for home. "I gather than you and Tuck didn't find anything."

He put the car in gear and then said, quietly, not exactly. He reached over the seat and handed me a small slip of paper. I looked down and saw one of Annette Gooden's business cards. As I took it from him, I said, "What?! She couldn't have been the one to leave it." My brain was trying to make sense of what I was seeing.

"Nope, she couldn't have, but someone who had one of her cards did." He glanced over at me. "The question is whether someone left it on purpose or by accident."

"On purpose?" I stared at the card for another moment before I understood what he was saying. "Wait, are you suggesting someone wanted to incriminate Annette but didn't know she was dead?"

He nodded. "I think it's a possibility," he said as he watched the road ahead and took the turn to St. Marin's. "It just seems pretty odd that given the situation her business card, of all things, would be at the place where we found our dogs."

I could tell he was still working through his theory, so I sat ruminating on my own. If someone had purposefully dropped Annette's card at the scene, they wanted us to think she was the one who kidnapped the dogs, maybe. That felt clunky and kind of obvious, but not everyone was a sophisticated criminal, I'd learned over the past couple of years. Still, why have us think that Annette had done this? What was the value in that?

Jared and I must have been puzzling on the same question because he said, "They must have wanted us to suspect her, maybe to deflect suspicion from someone else?"

A flash of insight flew through me. "Or to distract us?"

Jared glanced at me, and I saw him understand what I was saying. "All of us."

I nodded slowly even as he sped up and bent down to get his light. "Call Tuck," he said as he slapped the light onto the truck cab and flicked on the lights.

"We're at your store," Tuck said.

"What? Why?" My voice sounded shrill, even to me.

"Just meet us here," he said and hung up.

"They're at the store," I said, and Jared floored the gas. In two minutes, we were there, and the first thing I saw was the blue lights on Tuck's sedan flashing. The second was that the front window of my store had been completely shattered. "Oh no."

12

The first thing I thought was about my dogs and how grateful I was that they were at Rocky and Marcus's apartment. Then, I panicked. Full-blown, outright panic. Sit down on the sidewalk with a paperbag someone pulled from a trash can panic.

Mart came running when she saw me and dropped beside me instantly. "Harvey?"

I tried to acknowledge her presence with a nod, but I couldn't do anything but hold the bag, which smelled like Lu's tortilla chips, and force myself to fill it and then breath it in again like I'd seen people do on TV.

Eventually, as Mart held me against her on one side, my mom sidled up behind me and put her head on my back, whispering, and Henri took my other side and pressed her body against mine, I started to feel a calming in my chest. Cate and Elle sat down on the sidewalk in front of me, and each of them held one of my hands. Together, we breathed, and eventually, I lifted my head from the bag and sighed.

Cate leaned forward and put her hands on my face. "We've got you, Harvey. We got you."

Around me, my friends' bodies pushed closer, and something about their warmth and energy let me relax enough to speak. "Thank you," I said. "Thank you." I couldn't say more, but I knew they knew I meant that they had all my gratitude in the world.

Symeon leaned over and whispered something in Mart's ear. "Glass repair is on the way," she said to me. "They'll be here all night to help everyone."

I paused a moment. "Everyone?"

Henri tugged me tighter to her. "Four other businesses, including Max's, were vandalized tonight. All of them had their front windows broken."

Inside my body, a swirl of relief and sadness moved through me. I wasn't the only one targeted, and yet, more damage had been done to my lovely town. I couldn't revel in that.

"Who else?" I said as I forced myself to a squat and then, with help, stood up.

"The salon and the pet spa," Jared said as he made his way between my friends and wrapped an arm around my waist. "All had their front windows broken."

"But not yours?" I said, turning to Elle. "Your store is safe."

Elle nodded. "It seemed like they were focused only on your side of the street. Nothing over my way was touched."

I nodded, and even that small movement made me feel a little woozy. I looked up at Jared. "Is it okay if we go inside?"

"Yes, we'll just stay over in the café while the team finishes processing." He met my eyes and then led me to the door. "It's all going to be okay, Harvey," he whispered before pressing a kiss to my forehead.

I nodded because I believed him, but nothing in my body was ready to affirm that idea yet.

Rocky emerged from the backroom of the café with two carafes and set them on the counter. "Free coffee for everyone," she said. "Cinnamon rolls are on the way."

I heard a few groans from around the room as people took in that Rocky's mom was bringing her absolutely amazing, home-baked rolls. They alone would make this whole night better, at least for some people.

"Do we know anything?" Mom said as she slid a mug of coffee so light it was mostly cream in front of me.

Jared shook his head. "As far as we can tell, the rocks that were used were just regular field stones, something anyone could pick up from almost any yard around here. No notes. No other damage."

After a brief silence where we all, presumably, let the randomness of everything sink in, Marcus said, "So we are thinking that having the dogs kidnapped was a distraction from having someone here on Main Street, right?"

"Exactly our theory, Marcus," Tuck said as he and Lu made their way over. "There is method to this madness. Someone wanted to do this," he gestured to my shattered front window, "without being seen. The question is why."

I slumped back in my chair and closed my eyes for a moment as I tried to slow my thoughts enough to seize on one. But when that didn't happen, I did what I probably needed to do more: I just listened to myself. As I took some deep breaths, I let my thoughts swirl, noting each one as it came by but not trying to weave anything into something bigger. Immediately, I felt calmer, and when I opened my eyes, I had an idea.

"Can I look around?" I said as I stood up slowly. "See if anything was taken?"

"Please," Tuck said. "That is what we're asking all the shopowners to do."

"Who's doing it for the pet spa?" Cate asked as we made our way into the main part of the store. "I mean, Penelope is dead."

Tuck nodded. "We called in Sheila and Caro. They're with one of the Easton Deputies looking now."

I made my way toward the front window and took a deep

breath when I saw the huge shards of glass on my dogs' beds. But before I could think about the worst case scenario, I moved on, looking carefully at all the cat books in the window to see if anything was missing. But nothing was.

"You refilled the display?" I asked Marcus as the amoeba of people followed my lead as I began to walk through the store.

"Yep, before we closed Thursday. I wanted it to look fresh and good for the weekend."

I smiled at him. "Thanks." For several minutes, we wandered through the store en masse and studied the shelves and racks to see if we noticed anything missing. But the truth was, if someone had stolen a book, we probably wouldn't notice until inventory.

Fortunately, that was the next day, so we'd know sooner than usual. "You see anything?" I asked Marcus and Rocky as we stopped in front of the bookstore register.

"Nothing out of the ordinary," Marcus said and Rocky agreed. "Inventory will tell though."

"Right." I stared around my store. "I'm going to stay and help with that."

Jared looked at me, and momentarily, I thought he was going to object but instead he smiled. "I'll be on duty all night myself, so I'd rather you be here than home alone."

"That settles it," Bear said as he headed toward the café. "It's an inventory slumber party."

"Can I join in?" a woman's voice said, and I turned to see Rocky's mom coming through the door, her hair perfectly styled and her attire impeccable, even at 1am.

"Of course you can," I said as I hugged her neck and deftly swooped the platter of cinnamon rolls of her hand. "As long as I can have one of these."

She grinned. "Of course. Boys," she said as she turned to Walter, Luke, and Marcus. "There are two more trays in the car. Please fetch them."

"Yes, ma'am," the three said in unison.

"Let's set up right here," Rocky said after giving her future mother-in-law a kiss on the cheek.

Soon enough, we had a banquet of coffee, coffee fixings, and cinnamon rolls before us, and despite the ache in my joints that always appeared when I was sleep-deprived, I felt pretty alert. And the truth was, I couldn't imagine any of us being able to sleep that night, not after this much excitement in one day. "Might as well make the most of it?" I said, mostly to myself.

My dad heard me though, and said, "That's the spirit, Harvey." He kissed my cheek. "Do you want me to go get the dogs?"

I glanced toward the front window where a team of people were holding a sheet of glass on suction cups as they moved it toward my store.

"Looks like things will be safe for them soon, so yeah. Do you mind?" I asked.

"Not at all. I'll take your mother. Let you have a few minutes to organize everyone without her help." He winked at me.

My stress eased just a bit with that wink. There was something simply safe and open about knowing people so well that you can love them and save them – and others- from them without having to think too hard about it. "Thanks, Dad," I said before taking a huge bite of a cinnamon roll.

While Mom and Dad took Rocky's key to get our pups, Luke ran to their house to get Sasquatch – "he absolutely cannot miss this," Luke said. And so it was that a half-hour later, Marcus and I had gridded off the store and assigned pairs of people to take inventory. Marcus had already printed out the stock lists, so he divided those by section and handed them out.

Now, all everyone had to do was go through the shelves and check off each book that was there.

"If you feel like you can alphabetize as you go, please do," Marcus said. "But if that gets confusing, remember our main purpose here is inventory. We need to know what we have, and what we don't."

Heads around the store bobbed, and after another fortifying cup of coffee and, for many, a second cinnamon roll, everyone buddied up and headed to their section to start tracking books.

In a typical store, people are counting numbers of items, and that happened in a bookstore too, but because we only had one or two copies of most books, the most important thing was to track what titles we actually had, which had been misplaced or perhaps stolen. This made the process even more tedious than at, say, a pharmacy, because you weren't getting massive numbers of shampoo bottles to count. Here, you were simply looking for one copy of a book.

That was a particularly challenge in the children's section, so I had assigned Walter and Stephen to work there. In almost every way, they bucked the stereotype of white, cis, gay men, but in this one – attention to detail and appearance – they typified it. By the time they were done with the children's books, the space would be completely organized, tidy, and counted.

Marcus and I had partnered ourselves to do the front end inventory since it required us to have the master list of books and find single titles in various sections. That task was much easier for us since we knew the inventory most intimately. Plus, it had the added advantage of putting us near the front of the store so that I could keep an eye on the window replacement and the dogs.

"Looks like they've got it in," Marcus said as he held the spines of Jesmyn Ward's new book out so I could count them.

My total taken, I made my note on the book list and then

turned toward the window. "It does. How anyone can do that job without having a nervous breakdown, I don't understand." Just the idea of potentially breaking a piece of glass worth hundreds of dollar was enough to get my heart racing again, but add in that you could really hurt yourself or someone else, I couldn't even imagine.

"Agreed," Marcus said as he took the list and pointed to the next table we needed to count. "But the dogs are thoroughly entertained. "

After Pickle, Elle, and Henri carefully cleaned all the glass out of the window and the dog beds, they had put the pooch's spots back in their window and laid a treat on each of them. So when Mom, Dad , and Lucas returned with all four pups, they had immediately gone to the beds and laid down with their noses pointed toward the work crew. "Why do I think those four might have mastered the art of sleeping and watching at the same time?"

"I wouldn't doubt it," Marcus said. "So here's a question," he paused to count the stack of *Somehow* by Anne Lamott that I held out to him, "I know we think that the dogs were kidnapped as a distraction so that someone could do this." He waved the booklist toward the street outside. "But what if they also wanted the dogs away? Wanted to be sure Mayhem and Taco weren't in the store?"

"Why would they care? Someone who would do this doesn't care about whether a coupel animals get hurt?" I said, my anger welling up again.

Marcus took the books from my hands and put them back on the table beside me. "Are we sure?" He studied my face.

"So you think someone dognapped Mayhme and Taco to protect them?" I was finding this far-fetched, but then another thought came to me. "Or maybe they didn't want them barking?"

"That's possible, too. And maybe it's all three things – the person wanted everyone gone from the street, the dogs safe, and the potential for them to bark to be removed?" Marcus's eyebrows were near his hairline, the way they always were when he got really excited about something.

I took a deep breath and thought about his theory. "I suppose it's possible," I said, and even as I spoke, I felt that familiar squiggle of an idea coming together. "Next?" I said, determined now to finish the inventory and make something good come of tonight's mess.

WITHOUT FOUR HOURS, we had the entire store inventoried, and so with just a few hours before daylight, Stephen issued everyone a challenge. "If you've got it in you, let's clean the store completely before we close up. That way, on Monday, Harvey and Marcus come to a store that is sparkling and ready."

I smiled at him. "That's really nice, Stephen, but you all don't have to do that."

"Are you kidding me?" Bear said. "I have all day to sleep and watch football, and this gives me the perfect excuse. If you send me home now, Harvey, Henri will have me weeding by afternoon."

"it's true," Henri said. "Give us an excuse to laze an entire Sunday away Harvey."

I laughed and had to admit the idea sounded pretty amazing. "Okay, let's do it."

"You and I are not cleaning, though," Marcus said. "We are updating the inventory." When I raised one eyebrow at him, he said, "Might as well make the backend as clean as the front?"

"And you don't think we'll make mistakes given that we've been up all night?" I asked.

"Are you sluggish or sleepy?"

I thought a minute and realized I was the opposite – totally wired. "No, you're right. Let's do this."

I'm not normally a details person, but the ordering of things, of correcting our list was always something I enjoyed. Putting something right, I guess.

I was just about to say that to Marcus, to tell him I was really glad he suggested we finish this when that squiggle of something became a full blown thought and I blurted out, "You're totally right. I know who did it."

Marcus stared at me for a long minute and then, probably because he'd worked with me and my wild brain long enough, he made the lateral leap and said, "You know who broke the windows?"

I nodded. "And who killed Penelope. Get Jared."

He didn't hesitate and before I could say another word, he was out the front door and sprinting up the dawnscaped street to find my husband.

So it was that as the sun climbed up over my building and turned Main Street in St. Marin's a glowing orange, that I solved the murder of Penelope Greer. This was my poetic thought as I drank my ninth cup of coffee and finished the inventory update while I waited for Jared to arrive.

It didn't take long, and in the way that things can only happen occasionally, I finished the inventory, my friends finished cleaning, and Marcus returned with Tuck and Jared at the same time. That kind of serendipity feels portentous, at least when you've gotten married, rescued your dogs, and had your store vandalized all in a 24-hour period. Add in sleep-deprivation and syncronicity of that sort begins to feel like magic.

Perhaps that's why I didn't hem or haw or second-guess myself when I told Jared that I knew who had killed Penelope, kidnapped our dogs, and broken the store front windows. "I know I'm right," I said.

My husband stared at me for a long minute before looking at his boss and then back at me. "How do you know?" he asked.

It was only at this moment that my brain fully understand both the intensity of my caffeine high and the depths of my exhaustion and locked itself up in a temporary stall that must have looked, to everyone watching me, like I had gone into a catatonic seizure for a minute.

But fortunately, the adrenaline of having some answers kicked my neurons into gear for a last burst of insight, and I said, "Well, I don't know, except that I do know. I mean, I think I know. No, I'm sure I know."

Mart stepped forward and put her hands on my arms. "Breathe."

I took a deep breath.

"Now tell us," she said and stepped back into the huddle of my friends that had gathered around me at the register counter.

"Okay, it's something that Marcus said about the person who broke my window wanting to be sure the dogs were safe that got me thinking. What if that was true? What if the people who did this really cared about animals?"

Jared nodded at me and smiled. "Go on."

"So what if all of tonight's events – the dog napping, the window breaking – what if they were all staged so that someone could break into the dog spa and take something without it looking like that store was the focus?"

Tuck cleared his throat. "So you think someone did all of this just to get something from a pet grooming place?"

I could hear the skepticism in his voice, but he wasn't dismissing me so I went on. "Not just a pet grooming place, but a murder scene."

I tried not to gloat as I saw a flash of recognition cross the sheriff's face. "You think the murderer left something behind and needed to go back and get it?"

I nodded. "I do, and I think I know who it was."

. . .

IF YOU HAD BEEN DRIVING through St. Marin's Maryland on that Sunday morning about 5:30am, you would have been a full entourage of bedraggled people in wedding attire heading down Main Street like some sort of strange music video flash mob thing.

Most of the police presence was gone by then, so we probably looked like some sort of vigilante group on our way to proclaim justice, but with cell phones and dog leashes not pitchforks and torches. And if we hadn't all been so tired and strung out from a really wild few days, we might have thought better of our procession because of the fact that the people who usually processed this way were intent on harm and oppression.

But this morning, we were over-cafffeinated, hopped up on cinnamon roll sugar, and excited that maybe we had an answer to what was now two murders in our town. So march we did, albeit slowly, up to the pet spa, where Tuck ceremoniously and gently removed the crime scene tape and let us file into the tiny lobby of the building.

"Alright, Harvey," he said, "we've already carefully gone over the building, but if you promise to keep your hands to yourself, you can look around."

I nodded and dutifully shoved my hands into the pockets of my wedding dress that I had insisted were necessary. Clearly, I was right. Then, I began walking through the front of the spa, stepping over shards of broken glass that were yet to be cleaned up and moving, slowly, toward the front register.

"The money is gone out of the register, right?" I said even as I looked into the empty open drawer.

"Right," Jared said. "There wasn't any money in the register at the time of the murder."

"None at all," Cate said. "That's weird."

"Not really," Mart added. "We only keep a few bills in the register at the winery because most people pay by card now." She thought a minute. "But there wasn't any at all?"

Tuck shook his head. "Nope, we made a note because a business with no cash did seem very strange."

I sighed. "So let's assume," I looked over at Jared and then Tuck, "just go with me for a minute. Let's assume that the murderer took any cash in the register with them at the time of the murder. Whatever was there – a lot or a little."

Mart and Cate were nodding, so I gathered that made sense to them.

"So if that was the case, it wasn't the money they came back for." I felt a little bit like one of those mystery detectives who strung the audience along while she worked her theory, but in this case, I was just working out my theory, not trying to prove my prowess. "There must have been something else here that was worth stealing then, something they wouldn't have thought of at the time."

I bent over and looked under the counter. Extra register tape. One of those zipper bank envelopes everyone uses for deposits. A pen and some paper clips. Nothing else. I stood up and thought about our register, what we kept nearby. Much of the same stuff, but we also had bags, which would be necessary here since they didn't sell any products.

I closed my eyes and let the image of our register form behind them. I could see the cubbies to the left with all our various bags in them, the lower shelf with register tape, the stapler, a roll of transparent tape, and a stapler. My mental eye scanned up, and I saw the clipboard with our mailing list sign-up on it. My eyes flew open.

"Their appointment book." I glanced down again. "Where is the appointment book?"

Jared took a few steps toward me. "What appointment book? They have software to manage their appointments." He closed the distance between us and powered on the computer. With a few key strokes, he had a calendar app open on the screen. "See?"

I looked carefully at what he had pulled up. "I do, but when I was here booking my appointment for Taco and Mayhem, Sheila used an actual appointment book." I held my hands up to show something the size of a sheet of paper. "Covered in some red leather-like fabric."

Tuck nodded. "Alright, that we have not seen." He wrote something in his small notebook. "Anything else?"

I bent down to look under the register again. "Not that I notice," I finally said. "But that appointment book—"

Jared interrupted me. "We'll find it, Harvey. Thank you," he said and held out his hand. "Now, I think we all need to get some sleep." He turned to his boss. "You got this?"

"Yes, everyone," Tuck turned to face the group of people still gathered in the lobby. "Let's go home and rest. We'll regroup at 6 at Harvey and Jared's place." He turned to us. "If that's okay."

"Totally okay," I said. "Potluck. Bring whatever you want." I announced as I stifled a huge yawn. "But first, everyone sleep."

13

W hen I woke up eight hours later, it was 4 in the afternoon, and I was fairly sure I had traveled to another dimension while I slept. It took me a long time to figure out where I was given the way the light entered the room and the fact that I was, somehow, upside down in the bed. I pried myself to a sitting position and looked around, finally orienting myself to our bedroom and the bed too. I gave my head a little shake and then rubbed the considerable sleep from my eyes before that Jared wasn't still next to me, as he had been when I lay down.

"Jared?" I called.

"In the kitchen," he said. "Want me to bring you coffee?"

The thought was tempting, but two things held me back on the delivery. First, I was now aware that it was late afternoon, and I could not afford to be awake another night. And secondly, I really, really needed to pee. "No, thanks. I'll be down in a minute."

After a short trip to the bathroom and a very precarious venture down the stairs with four dog escorts, I made it to the kitchen. "Remind me why I thought we should bring all these guys home."

Jared looked up from his phone and said, "You said they had been so excited about their slumber party that you didn't want to break it up."

"Clearly, that was my fatigue talking." I walked to the back door and opened it. "Out, all of you. Go do your business and stay out there for a while. You four have gotten enough sleep for eight dogs."

"And you've had enough sleep for only half a person," my husband said as he pulled me close and tight. "Do you feel better?"

I took a deep breath and thought about his question. "Yes, some. But I also hurt all over and really just want to lay on our couch and doze through something pointless."

"Well, let's do that then. I'll tell everyone that we're rain-checking the potluck." He already had his phone in his hand.

"No, wait. Did Tuck make any arrests today?" I asked, hoping that he had with every tired fiber of my being.

Jared shook his head and then sighed. "The judge issued the warrants, but no, no arrest."

It was my turn to sigh. "Okay then, we need to meet up then. Maybe as a collective we can figure out next steps." I slumped into a chair by the kitchen island.

"You realize," Jared said as he came around and stood beside me, "that solving this case isn't your job, even if your store was targeted, right?"

I nodded. "I do, and a big part of me wants to just leave it to you and Tuck and get back into bed." Before he could say anything, "But the part of me that wants justice for Annette and even for Penelope won't let the other part sleep again until we finish this up."

Jared pulled me against his side. "Okay," he said quietly.

"Also, I want this to be over for you," I said as I slid back and looked up at him. "Both of us have carried this situation through our wedding weekend. I'm ready for it to be done."

"Me, too," he said. "Me too." He poured two mugs of coffee and handed me one. When I tried to decline, he said, "It's decaf. I'm not a monster."

I smiled and took the creamy sweet drink from him. "You absolutely are not." As I made my way to the sofa, I said, "Want to watch something completely ridiculous for me until our friends come?"

"Of course," I do. So for the next two hours, we watched the first ever season of *The Bachelor*, and it was bad in so many ways that it was entirely perfect. By the time our friends came bearing various casseroles and desserts and had, wisely, not brought a fresh vegetable between them, I was longing to talk about the murders again because I could not stand to look at the terrible evening gown designs of the 1990s anything. So many ruffles.

A PLATE full of macaroni and cheese, some sort of cream of mushroom and beef casserole, and two pieces of cake later, I was completely full, entirely ready to sleep again, and determined that I was not going to do that until we wrapped up this case.

"Okay, so here's what's happened while we've all been snoozing today," Tuck began as soon as I shut off the music and gave him a nod. "We have searched the suspects' houses, and we have not yet recovered the appointment book. We assume, then, that they have it with them." His voice was very terse, and I could almost hear the exhaustion in his words.

A long silence permeated the room, and I wondered if everyone else was struggling as much as I was to put ideas together. "And you haven't found Sheila and Caro yet?"

"What?" Cate said. "Are they the suspects?"

Jared looked over at me and then turned his gaze back to Cate. "Yes." He didn't elaborate. He didn't explain.

"What about Toggle and that grumpy vet guy?" Mart asked.

"They're still suspects, too, but it's unlikely they would have known about the appointment book," Tuck answered. "Please, everyone, give us a chance to explain everything."

Everyone, including me, settled back into their chairs and looked at Tuck. "So the fact that the appointment book is missing is quite significant. It was there when we took the crime scene photos after Ms. Greer's murder, so we know it wasn't stolen at that time. And since the spa has been locked up and sealed with tape, we know no one took it in the intervening days."

Mart started to raise her hand with a question, but Tuck gave her a raised eyebrow and she quickly put her hand down. "WE also know that no one entered the spa between the time we sealed the spa and today because we have surveillance on the building." He didn't elaborate, but I was really curious about how our tiny police department could afford a stake-out or some technology to keep an eye on a building.

Fortunately, my husband knew me well, and he said, "We used game cameras. One at each entrance. It would have recorded anyone entering via door or window."

I stifled a giggle, not because that wouldn't work – it was actually pretty genius – but because it was such a Southern small-town thing to do. I could picture the camo-covered boxes tucked into corners by each door now. I wondered how many stray cats they had caught on film, a question I'd have to ask Jared later.

I saw Pickle wiggling in his seat the way a young child does when they know the answer to a question the teacher asked but have been told they talked too much. He was putting things together.

Tuck gave him the same look he had given Mart, and the

man sat still immediately. Tuck would have made a great kindergarten teacher. "Toggle and Dr. Stoltzfus are still on our list, as I said." He looked over at Pickle again. "But they have no reason to know about the second means of tracking customers, and since that seems to have been the purpose of all of tonight's shenanigans, we have to favor the two people who did: Sheila and Caro, the spa employees."

I was clearly tired because I had to cough down another laugh at the way Tuck's voice had gotten super formal and crisp. He was in full sheriff mode now.

"And before you ask," he shot a look to Henri, who had leaned forward, "we do not know exactly why the appointment book is so important. From what we know of it, it contains the same information as in the computer records. Yet, we clearly are missing something because it was worth all this mayhem." He looked over at our dog sleeping soundly by the fireplace. "No offense."

That little interchange broke the room's tension, and everyone started talking at once. Apparently, Tuck decided he had shared enough of the police investigation with this group of "citizens," because he sat down and opened a beer.

For a few minutes, everyone rabbled to everyone else about their theories and motives and such. But eventually, the room settled again, and Lucas said, "What do you need us to do?"

Tuck smiled over his beer. "Just keep an eye out for Sheila or Caro. If you see them, call us. Don't intervene." He let that last sentence hang in the air. "Seriously."

Jared bumped my knee with his own, a gentle reminder that this admonition applied to me, too.

I nodded, too tired to even think about sleuthing at the moment. "Thank you for coming, everyone." I stood up and smiled. "Thank you for everything. Now, as a very tired bride, could I ask you to please clean your dishes, return the furniture to its original position, and go home."

A small chuckle went around the room, and then everyone was up and moving with plates and cups, and soon the house was back in order and empty except for Tuck and Lu, Jared and me. "Harvey, I know you're exhausted, but I do have one more question. What else can you remember about that appointment book?"

I sighed and then rallied the last of my energy before closing my eyes and picturing the scenes at the spa when I'd first made the dogs appointments and then when I'd gone back to get them. "I definitely remember the book being there when I scheduled with them. They wrote down all the details in the book, including my phone number and address." I squinted, trying to remember more. "Then, when I came back for the dogs, they put all my payment information into a section at the back." My eyes flew open. "That book was full of people's bank and credit card information."

Jared sighed. "Great."

"We definitely have to recover that book if only to prevent the identity theft of a lot of people." Tuck rubbed his bald head. "We can use the computer records to track everyone down in the meantime and let them know to bolster their internet security."

Tuck stood up, and by "'we' I mean the folks from Easton. You and I need some sleep, Jared, and so do our wives." Tuck smiled at us then. "Congratulations. I know it wasn't the wedding weekend of your dreams, but somehow, it seems fitting doesn't it?"

I couldn't argue with him there. Somehow, I did seem to get mixed up in a lot of murders. Tonight, though, the only thing I was getting mixed up in was my sheets.

THE NEXT MORNING, I was so groggy that I could barely get dressed and get the dogs leashed for the walk to work. But even though Jared offered to drive me on his way in, I knew I needed the walk both for my mental and physical health and because if I didn't take it, I was going to be useless at the store.

Fortunately, by the time the three of us reached All Booked Up, my head had cleared and I was even a little excited about the state of the shop. Everything was in it's place, and we now had a very accurate inventory that would mean we didn't say we had a book for a customer when we really didn't. Saving ourselves those tiny moments of frustration was a nice bonus for the start of the week.

When I walked through the door, the smell of brewing coffee and books immediately eased some of the tension in my chest. I loved my home with Jared, but this place was mine – not exclusively, of course – but in a very real sense, I was the one who had made this place into being. For that reason, it always felt safe to me. Today was no different.

After a quick word with Rocky to thank her for everything again and get my vanilla latte, I joined Marcus at the register. "So what do you have in mind?"

He looked over at the front window, which looked totally normal except for the stack of cat books that had been put in one corner. "New display?"

"Agreed," I said. "What's your vision?" I had long ago learned that while I might have concepts for window themes, Marcus was the real creative when it came to displays.

He paused a minute as he studied the front of the store and then he grinned. "What if we did a wedding theme in this window?" He pointed to where the glass had just been replaced. "And use some of the items from the window we did for you and Jared."

I smiled and nodded. He wasn't done, and I knew it.

"Then, over in the café, what if we did one on art, display some of our pricier books and make a sign inviting everyone in to see Toggle's piece here." He looked over at me and frowned.

"Unless we don't want to draw attention to her work since she's a murder suspect."

I had been thinking exactly the same thing, but I didn't want to be that way. "I'm not always the biggest fan of the American legal system, but I think there's something really powerful about innocent until proven guilty. Let's do it."

Marcus smiled. "Great. Want to grab some art books and I'll get to work on the wedding stuff." He winked at me. "Unless you'd like to do more wedding planning."

"No, thank you," I said. "I'm all set. Art books it is."

Cate and Henri were really the art experts, but I decided that I was going to do a display of all the art books I loved most. I pulled *Gifts from the Fire*, a beautiful photographic collection of late 19th and early 20th century ceramics, *Art of Native America*, a collection of various art from tribes across the continent, and finally, *Rural Modern*, a collection of artistic works that represent the countryside. Seeing that I was clearly on an American bent that day, I expanded my theme, and before I knew it, I had a collection of 25 gorgeous art books that would be perfect in the window either to show their covers or opened to a beautiful spread of images.

When I was finished, I was so excited that I decided to do something we hadn't done since the store opened and pulled all the remaining art books off the shelves and began cleaning behind them. It was a luxury to do so, and I was pleased to see that the shelves weren't actually that dirty.

I was just beginning to return the books to the shelves when I heard the bell over the door ring. "Harvey, people are here for you," Marcus called, and I stepped out from behind the shelves.

There, in the middle of my store, stood Sheila and Caro, and they looked, well, fine. Not resplendent. Not bedraggled. Just fine. Sheila was wearing a long trench over a flowerprint dress, and Caro had on jeans and a blouse with what looked like an art portfolio bag flung over one shoulder. "Hi, Ladies.

How can I help you? I haven't seen you in a few days. Everything okay?"

Sheila nodded. "Yeah, considering. We went into Easton for the weekend, just needed a break."

Behind the two women, I could see Marcus texting furiously, and I was grateful that he was on top of things since I didn't think I could do much more at the moment than keep the women talking.

"Well, what brings you in today. Looking for something to read?" I asked, hoping I sounded more casual than I felt.

"Actually, yeah," Caro said. "We're kind of at a loss about what to do while we wait to see if we can open the shop again. And after last night's vandalism—"

I interrupted, "Oh yes, I'm sorry that happened to you, too. I just don't know who would do such a thing. Do you have any ideas?" The southern in my accent was getting much richer, which it did anytime I was acting or lying, but I hoped these two wouldn't notice.

"No," Sheila said. "That was just so cruel." She sighed. "But I guess it could have been worse. At least no one was hurt." She glanced over her shoulder at the front of the store, where Mayhem and Taco were surprisingly upright and watching us.

The dogs didn't seem scared, but they were definitely paying attention to these two women in a way they didn't attend to most customers, unless those people were carrying treats. For me, that was enough evidence to prove that our theories were correct – Caro and Sheila had not only killed Penelope Greer but had also kidnapped our dogs and vandalized the store to get the appointment book back.

But of course, we had no way to prove that without that appointment book. I was just going to have to keep them here until Tuck or Jared came to arrest them. "Well, would you like me to direct you to anything in particular? What do you like to read?"

Sheila smiled. "Do you mind if we just browse? We might get a coffee and relax in the café."

"Of course," I said. "Enjoy and let us know if we can help."

My brain was racing with what to do, but I figured if they were calm enough to just stroll in here then they'd be calm enough to stay as long as we didn't alarm them. So I went back to what I was doing after giving Marcus the nod to stay out front and keep an eye on the two women.

As soon as I stepped behind the bookshelves and bent to pick up the first stack of books to place them on the shelves, my phone buzzed in my pocket. It was Jared texting. "I'm on my way. Are they still there?"

"Yes, in the café. They seem relaxed." I withheld the overly polite impulse to say, "No rush," because that was a ridiculous thing to say to a police officer whose prime murder suspects were sipping lattes.

"Be there in five," he replied, and I slipped the phone back into my pocket and returned to shelving books.

I was into the middle of my fifth heavy stack of titles when something caught my eye as I fronted the spines of the book to the edge of the shelf. There, right between a Manet and a Monet collection was a red book. There were no words on the spine, and it was a sort of bumpy texture that wasn't typical on modern books.

My heart started to race, and I pulled it off the shelf. "Calendar," it said on the front, and I didn't even have to open it to know what it was. They had stashed Penelopes appointment book here, in a building full of books, and now they were here to get it.

Just then, I heard a rustling behind me and turned to see Sheila there with a knife held out in front of her. "I'll be needing that, Harvey. Thank you."

I turned to run the other direction but stopped short when I saw Caro at the other end of the shelf. I was boxed in.

For a brief moment, I considered scaling the nearest shelf and running, Enola Holmes style, across the bookshelves to the front door, but then I remembered I was nearly 50, not limber at all, and definitely not fast. "Why do you need it?" I said as I glanced from Caro to Sheila and back.

Sheila shook her head and looked like she was going to cry. "I'm really sorry, Harvey. I didn't mean for it to come to this. We want to take over her business. Run it better, you know. Be kind to both the people and the animals."

"So you need her calendar to do that? Why?" I knew I was fishing for information, but I also knew that if I gave them this book they would just flee, although how far a list of local customers would go I wasn't sure. I wasn't sure any of us were thinking very rationally at that moment.

Caro answered me. "Penelope didn't trust the internet, said someone might steal her customer's information if we put it in the computer, so we had to keep everything in here."

"Including credit card numbers," I said. "So you're going to use the book to steal from customers? How does that make you better than her?" I was studying Caro's face now. She didn't look quite as distraught as her friend.

"What?! No," Sheila shouted. "We just need the addresses and phone numbers so we can contact them when we get up and running again. We weren't going to use the credit card numbers at all."

I looked at the young woman who was now crying and then turned back to her accomplice. "Is that right, Caro? Is that all you had planned?"

Caro smiled just enough to make my bones ache. "Well, at first, yes, but then, well, who wants to give dogs baths all day for the rest of her life?"

Sheila gasped, and I turned back toward her, noticing that the knife had dropped to her side. Now was my chance. I bolted past Sheila, knocking her into the bookshelf as I went, and then, with the appointment book tucked against my chest like I was a running back on the way to the game-winning touchdown, I sprinted toward the front door, where I saw Jared and Tuck running toward me.

AT LEAST THIS is how I would tell the story to my friends later when we gathered at the bookstore for drinks after Sheila and Caro were arrested. I don't have any idea why I pulled in the football analogy – I hated the sport – but it had seemed apt at the time.

"I'm going to call you Ink Blitz from now on, Harvey," Bear said and sent the whole room into laughter. "Maybe you should join a PowderPuff team or something?"

"Powder Puff. How condescending," Cate said. "Join a rugby team, Harvey. You'd come out of the scrum with power."

I rolled my eyes and took another sip of my decaf latte. "Alright, enough. The football analogy was ill-advised, obviously. I'm just glad you two were there," I said as I squeezed Jared's hand and looked at Tuck. "What will happen now?"

"Well, they've been charged with murder. The district attorney thinks that between the fact that you found them standing over the body, the fact that they committed theft and vandalism to retrieve and then hide again the key piece of their plan, and their threat to you we have a good case."

"But why did they do it? Mart asked. She had come running into the store as soon as she heard what had happened and refused to leave my side all day.

"Well, that's what's interesting," Jared said. "For Caro, it was all about the money. She was really the mastermind, but she preyed on Sheila's love of animals to bring her in. For Sheila it was all about the dogs."

"I love dogs too," Mom said as she scratched Sidecar's ear, "but I'm not willing to kill a person for them."

"Me neither," I said. "But some people are, apparently." I bent down and scrunched one of Taco's ears until he moaned. "The thing is that the murder wasn't really necessary at all. Caro could have just stolen the book and left town, and Sheila could have easily warned customers about Penelope's attitude toward her client's pets."

"As if they even needed warning," Pickle added. "Her reputation was going to sink her business anyway."

I leaned back. "One question I still have. Why did they kill Annette Gooden?" I had been thinking about the beautiful, kind young woman all afternoon, and I just couldn't figure out how she had gotten mixed up in all this.

"That's the truly tragic part. She was just trying to help," Tuck said. "According to Sheila, Annette came by the day of the fundraiser for the cats and offered her grooming services at a very reduced rate if it would help Sheila and Caro get the business going again."

"Yep, apparently, she offered to set up a mobile dog wash station outside the shop on warm days and give free washes for anyone who booked an appointment in the spa," Jared said.

"Well, that just seems nice, doesn't it?" Henri said.

"You'd think so, but Caro convinced Sheila that Annette was trying to horn in on their business, and so they killed her," Tuck said.

"Oh, that's awful," Elle said. "All of this is just awful."

We sat quietly for a long moment, a show of respect of sorts for the women who had lost their lives so unnecessarily.

Finally, though, Lucas spoke up. "Well, what now? That store front is going to be empty, apparently, and we're down two pet groomers in the town. The tourists aren't going to like that."

"Oh, never fear, Dr. Stoltzfus has already assured us that he's going to open up a holistic spa at his clinic." Jared sighed. "He's kind of a jerk, but he means well. . . I think."

Symeon cleared his throat and said, "I hope this doesn't

sound terribly crass, but does that mean the space on Main is going to be up for lease?"

Tuck looked at him and nodded. "Talked to the owner today. He's putting out the ad first thing tomorrow and hoping to have a tenant by week's end, when the space will be clear."

Mart turned and looked at her fiancé. "Why are you asking?" She was squinting and smiling at him at the same time.

"No reason," he said. "No reason at all."

We were all too tired to push him, and besides, it seemed like this might be a discussion for Mart and Symeon alone. So I stood up and said, "It looks like these two," I glanced down at the two snoring dogs at our feet, "will be getting baths with the hose from now on."

At that, Mayhem lifted her head, gave her ears a shake, and then laid back down.

"Someone doesn't approve," Jared said.

"Someone doesn't get a vote," I replied before I slid down onto the floor and pulled both of the pooch's warm heads into my lap. "Good pups," I whispered. "Good pups."

THANK you so much for reading the ARC of this book. If you would be so kind as to review the book on Goodreads - https://www.goodreads.com/book/show/208873569-dog-eared-danger - and/or on Bookbub - https://www.bookbub.com/books/dog-eared-danger-st-marin-s-cozy-mystery-series-book-11-by-acf-bookens, I would greatly appreciate it. Reviews are not required but do make my heart happy. THANKS.

I WILL SEND out another email closer to the release date of April 23rd with link for the retailers. The book cannot be reviewed there until release day. THANKS again. - Andi